SEVERE

SEVERE

RÉGIS JAUFFRET

Translated from the French by
Joel Anderson

PRESS LIMITED

First published in the United Kingdom in 2013 by
Salammbo Press
39A Belsize Avenue
London NW3 4BN
www.salammbopress.com

Originally published in the French language as *Sévère*
by Éditions du Seuil, Paris
© Régis Jauffret and Éditions du Seuil, 2010

The moral right of Régis Jauffret to be identified as the
author of this work has been asserted in accordance with the
Copyright, Designs and Patents Act 1988

Thanks to Marie Auberger

A CIP catalogue record for this book
is available from the British Library

Cover design: Regis Allouet
Typeset by Tetragon, London

ISBN 978–0–9568082–4–0

SEVERE

Fiction shines like a torch. A crime will always remain obscure. The culprit is arrested, the motive revealed, they are judged, sentenced, but in spite of all this the shadow remains, like the darkness in the cellar of a house lit by sunlight. Imagination is a tool of knowledge, it looks from afar, it dives into the details as if it wanted to explore the very atoms, it twists the real, it stretches it to breaking point, it carries it along in its deductions filled with axioms that by their nature will never be proven.

Yes, but fiction does lie. It fills the chinks with the imaginary, with gossip, slander that it invents as things proceed, in order to drive the tale onwards, blow by blow. It is born of bad faith, just as some are born blue or completely idiotic. Anyway, it is often stupid. when logic slows right down, it is apt to vault over intelligence as if it were an obstacle. At such points, it ignores it, or even smashes its face in with a casual punch. Fiction enjoys sophism just as much as it enjoys the rudeness of Gargantua (who, like his father, was an inveterate scatologist), or Balzac's miserly, greedy *petits bourgeois*, or Homais (an apothecary and imbecilic scientist), or Madame Verdurin (a vulgar and notorious oaf), of all the boors that populate magnificent novels, clumsy pachyderms, diamonds that cross centuries and leave flabbergasted in their tombs the inhabitants of the past, who succeed one another with the regularity of underground trains.

In this book, I bury myself in a crime. I visit it, I photograph it, I film it, I record it, I mix it, I falsify it. I am a novelist, I lie like a murderer. I respect neither the living nor the dead, nor their reputations, nor morality. Especially not morality. As written by bourgeois conformists who dream of prizes and little castles, literature is a rogue. It advances, it destroys. That's its honour, its way of being honest, to leave behind nothing of a story that it has used to build a very little object full of pages, a file packed with bytes, a story to read in bed or standing on a rock facing the ocean, like the poet Chateaubriand lost in an idealised image.

I would not hesitate to slit your throat if you were a sentence that pleased me and that was ready to be inscribed in a novel as slim as my remorse at having bumped you off. I am a decent man, you can trust me with your cat, but writing is a weapon I like to use in the crowd. And when you've taught the crowd to read, it will just as easily kill your cat.

Nobody is ever dead in a novel. Because nobody exists within it. The characters are puppets full of words, spaces, commas, with the skin of a syntax. Death goes through them from one part to another, like air. They are imaginary. They never existed. Don't believe this story is real; it is I who invented it. If some people recognise themselves in it, they had better run a bath. Their head under the water, they will hear the beat of their heart. Sentences don't have one. They would be mad, those who think they are imprisoned in a book.

R.J.

I MET HIM ONE SPRING EVENING. I BECAME HIS mistress. I bought the latex suit he was wearing on the day he died. I acted as his sexual secretary. He introduced me to firearms. He gave me a revolver. I extorted a million dollars out of him. He took it back. I slaughtered him with a bullet between the eyes. He fell from the chair where I'd tied him up. He was still breathing. I finished him off. I went to take a shower. I picked up the shells. I put them in my bag with the revolver. I slammed the door of the apartment behind me.

The CCTV recorded me leaving the building at twenty-one thirty. I got in my car. A storm had broken on the far side of the lake. I drove through every red light. I went home. I told my husband I was going on a trip.

'You have a crazy look in your eyes.'

I slipped my hand inside his jacket. I took his wallet. I left him his licence and his identity card.

'Are you keeping the car?'

I dropped the key on the table.

'Is something wrong?'

He placed his hand on my shoulder.

'Stop.'

'At least tell me where you're going.'

I was going far away. Murderers go away. Time zones allow the clock to be turned back. To return to the time when nothing had yet taken place, to a country where the crime will not be committed.

'Call me a taxi.'

He obeyed, like an old soldier tired of challenging orders.

I got caught in the storm. I waited for the taxi with him, under his big umbrella.

'Call me when you get there.'

The car arrived. The driver got out to open the door for me.

'Take the umbrella.'

'The storm isn't going to follow me to the ends of the earth.'

He watched the car pull away, standing in the downpour, leaning on the umbrella like a walking stick.

I asked the driver to take me to Milan.

'That will cost you at least eight hundred euros.'

'Do you take American Express?'

'Yes.'

'Let's go.'

As we left town, I told him to stop by the side of the road. I walked to the river bank. I threw the shells and the revolver into the lake. I made the sign of the cross. I didn't believe in God any more than I believed in the lottery. Still, I sometimes bought a ticket when I was getting cigarettes. That night, I was in a situation where I needed to have luck on my side.

I got back in the car. The driver looked at me in the mirror. I felt the need to justify myself.

'I got rid of a bad memory.'

'At the bottom of the lake?'

I hadn't thrown them far. A bit like throwing a *boule*. I was fond of that revolver, I wanted there to be a chance of getting it back one day.

'I'll turn up the heating.'

I was wet. I was afraid I might catch cold, might have to put off this trip. I spread my clothes out on the seat. He looked away.

'Never seen a woman in her knickers before?'

It was too dark to see if he blushed.

We had beaten the storm. The road was dry.

Under pressure from his children and their mother, the police will remove the crime from their files. Prominent families don't like to publicise their troubles. They will send out a terse press release.

'Died of a heart attack at his home.'

■

If only he had denied me that million dollars, I would never have got a taste for money. I had barely felt the taste in my mouth when he confiscated it. He was too rich to realise that you can get attached to a million dollars just as you can get attached to a cat.

He didn't like cats. I had taken in a kitten that had come in through the window. One morning, it snuggled up to a pillow that was still warm from my cheek.

'Stupid bastard.'

After insulting it, he threw it. I heard it meowing in the bathroom. It had a broken tooth. I saw a bloodstain on the wall. It never got on the bed again. I had to put its basket and bowl under the cabinet where it had taken refuge. It was scared, even of me. In the end it ran away. I think I saw it a few days later. A pancake of white fur in the car park. He must have run it over with his Bentley.

He liked to kill animals. He paid a fortune for the right to hunt antelopes, hippopotamuses, lions, in African reserves where nervous tourists took photographs of them from the half-open windows of air-conditioned 4x4s. He took me to Tanganyika several times. We took his jet, and we camped in the savannah. The guide always said that one must slaughter a wounded animal. After the first bullet, I thought he was still alive. I finished him off so he wouldn't suffer.

THE DAY AFTER THE MURDER, HIS ASSISTANT WAS surprised that he wasn't at the office. His mobile was still in his jacket pocket. It vibrated with every message she left him, in the frozen silence of the room.

Before leaving, I had turned off the radiator. I had opened the window that looked out onto an interior garden. I had drawn the curtains, turned off the light. An improvised crypt, made out of respect for someone to whom I was once worth a million dollars.

His partner entered the apartment at around six in the evening. The concierge had let him in. He found a giant collapsed latex doll. Not a single stain on the white rug. The latex had closed up after the bullets entered. The suit was full of blood.

'I could see there was a man inside.'

A six-foot-four man with broad shoulders.

'I couldn't be sure it was him.'

He didn't dare open the zip to see his face. The concierge came into the room.

'It's freezing cold.'

'Get out.'

She hadn't noticed the body.

'The only light was the bedside lamp. I just saw that the curtain was torn.'

He was afraid to leave fingerprints. To breathe any longer in a room that would be scrutinised down to the level of its miasma. He slammed the door. He shoved the woman into the corridor. She banged against the wall. He pulled her by the arm to direct her towards the exit.

'Sir, you're hurting me.'

He pushed her in front of him like a crate. He was afraid that the doll would rise up and chase him like a Golem. He bumped into furniture and sculptures. A Giacometti statue fell from its plinth. He was rushing her so much, she cried out on the stairs.

She had left the key inside. The police had to call a locksmith. The mechanism of the lock was too complicated. He had to smash open the door with a jackhammer. The body was transported to the police forensic laboratory. The coroner told the hearing that he had cut the latex with a Stanley knife.

'It was as if I was removing him from a mould.'

The hood had prevented the head from shattering. The mortician only needed to block the hole piercing the forehead. They were able to show him, and to give his funeral elegy with the body on display. As if victims were always innocent. As if it was right to endure years of prison for such a fleeting act.

He died while loving. If I hadn't had his trust, he wouldn't have agreed to offer himself to me, blind and bound. He was too heavy for me to carry in my arms. Otherwise, I would have rocked him, revolver in hand. He would have sucked its opening like the teat of a bottle. I would have fed him with a bullet.

I relieved him of a life that was as brilliant and dark as the finish on his coffin. It was a predator's life, and his cynicism earned him the admiration of the financial press, swift to kneel before the crooks who lubricate their speculative capitalism, just as peasants used to kneel before their manure-producing pig. If victims were the ones being judged, they would often be given harsher sentences than their killers. The death sentence, once given as punishment to their murderers, would be reinstated for them.

He was supposed to marry me. I would have returned the million dollars on our wedding day. It would be back in our coffers again. I had needed that money as a token of love. For me, the transfer of funds was as touching as any proposition. When you are worth two billion euros, you can afford to give a ring to your betrothed.

After my arrest, his family stated that they didn't want the cash. If the courts ended up awarding it to them, they would even double the trifling sum and give it to the poor. He was never so generous with me. He was greedy, miserly, my husband even had to pay for the picnic I took when I left alone with him in his jet. My husband clothed me, fed me, provided my pocket money. He gave me a little country house in Avallon so I could isolate myself whenever I pleased.

He still loves me. He comes to visit me in prison twice a week. He has always been ready to sacrifice himself to satisfy my whims. Several years before the affair, he even agreed to exempt me from sexual relations.

'When I force myself to screw you, I feel like a prostitute.'

'I don't pay you.'

'You keep me.'

'I won't bother you any more, then, with conjugal obligations.'

'Let's sleep in separate rooms.'

'I like sleeping by your side.'

'I don't want you to be tempted.'

'I'll move into the spare room.'

By way of recompense, I kissed him on the neck.

'You will always be my best friend.'

I had been close to rich men, they reassure me. Money smells good, and these people give off a perfume of banks, of pink marble, of paintings by the great masters, of lounges as large as town squares, of fresh beds with sheets changed every day by maids, of hot swimming pools, steaming, overlooking the town in the frozen December air. And the scent of kerosene whose notes are perceived fleetingly as the jet tears off the tarmac, the leather of sedans, dressing rooms as spacious as boutiques, shelves loaded with cashmere, flannel suits in their covers, Italian shoes constructed around plaster replicas of their feet so as not to tire them with fittings. An odour that is even more irresistible than the pheromones emanating from perfect strangers in the arms of another.

I met him at the home of an antique-dealer friend. He often organised intimate dinners in his apartment, which was decorated like a cruise ship. On this occasion, he called in a few girls to be enjoyed after the coffee. That evening, there were four of us women, lined up in the kitchen in front of appetisers and large glasses of vodka. The cook did not speak to us, finding her role more respectable than ours. They ate alone in the mahogany dining room. We could hear them discussing the oil markets and the future of gas.

I had slept with the antique dealer every now and then. He often left his money-clip on the bedside table. As a courtesy, I would leave him a message. His response was always the same.

'Keep it all. Buy yourself some clothes.'

Three hundred euros, sometimes a bit more. The clip was made of gold, he must have bought them by the case. I gave them to my husband. He sold them to make some cash. He perked up when he saw me in a new dress that he hadn't paid for.

'See – I don't keep you as much as all that.'

He deduced from this that he deserved a hug. He would scratch at my door at night. I had to remind him of the rules to get him to go back to sleep in the spare room.

A physiotherapist doesn't make much, and the herbal medicine business he had set up in 1998 gave him nothing but grief. I also entertained other men who casually emptied their wallets into my bag as they left. I didn't profit from this money, I was like those beanpoles who stuff themselves and are still skin and bone. Men's money evaporated. Boutiques drank it up like the sand the drizzle. I continued to cost him and to increase his overdraft with every little bite.

The idea of a million dollars was his.

'If he agrees, it means he truly loves you.'

Such a sum is blinding, it cannot be looked at directly. A sacred sum, an untouchable sum. You don't squander a token of love.

My husband warned me that the value would dwindle bit by bit.

'Inflation eats away at money.'

Even diminished, it would have retained for me all of its purity, with its six blazing zeroes. At any moment, I could have claimed it in bundles of notes or in gold. Gold ingots or coins spread out on my bed, glistening like the flashes of light that appeared sometimes in his eyes when he desired me, when he was dying of love, when he illuminated me with all his hatred. That money was a minuscule morsel of him. A fragment ripped from his fortune, a mouthful of flesh cut from a living body. A discomfort he accepted as proof of his passion.

But he quickly regretted this sacrifice, he couldn't bear to leave this wound open for very long. Money cures money wounds, and if he managed to get his hands on it again, his moment of negligence would be wiped forever from his memory.

The driver asked if I did any sport.

'I work out a bit, myself.'

I replied as little as possible to his questions. I saw that he glanced into the rear-view mirror. He was examining me.

'Why are you looking at me? I've put my clothes back on.'

'I'm looking at the road.'

I turned my head. The road was black.

'I'm tired. Wake me up when we arrive.'

I closed my eyes to make him think I was sleeping. I heard the storm approaching. I opened my eyelids slightly. There was lightning all around us. I would have liked to have been struck by lightning, and to stay in hospital cocooned by nurses who would stop the police from interrogating me.

I said to myself that memory is a source of worry. If only I could have eaten this memory, and expelled the murder in the natural way.

We didn't dare leave the kitchen to ask how long we needed to wait before being put to use. We were a bit drunk. One of the girls was Ukrainian. The shopkeeper had called me the day before to make sure I invited her.

'She needs to be there at eight.'

'I don't know if she'll want to. She's not a whore.'

'She's like you, she's a *demi-mondaine.*'

I found that word elegant. But the whole room burst out laughing when I used it at my trial to counter the prosecution, who were calling me a call-girl.

They came to get us at around midnight. The shopkeeper took the Ukrainian, and a brunette I hadn't seen before.

The fourth was a girl who I don't remember at all, since she was neither ugly nor pretty. She stayed in the kitchen drinking. In reserve, like a piece of bread from the day before that you don't want to throw away in case it's needed.

He pointed at me. Like a warder singling out a prisoner walking the yard. I followed him down the corridor. He spoke into my ear with his deep voice. I let myself be seduced. We came out into a bedroom with a bed lit up by four spotlights. Like a boxing ring.

He got undressed as he entered. I removed my eye make-up with wipes. I don't like leaving a man's arms with my eyes caked in mascara. He waited for me, sitting calmly on the edge of the bed. I went towards him naked, taking little steps like a mechanical toy. He did a twisting motion with his fingers to signal that I should turn around. I heard the sound of a condom packet being torn. I heard him stand up. He placed his fingers on my breasts to scratch them. I felt his hard penis on my back. A painful penetration like a massive kick. I found him discourteous not to have asked my permission before entering me like that. I pulled free.

Face to face, standing on my tiptoes, I slapped him as hard as I could. I saw the red imprint of my hand double, triple, multiply on cheeks bearing the blue shadow of his beard. He liked it, and pushed his head towards me like a female primate sticking out her rear. He moved back, rattled by the orgasm. He let himself fall flat onto the bed.

We went back to his place to sleep. I woke up tied to the bed. The room was white. The sun was coming in through gaps in the roller blind. On a chair, my black dress bound up with my bra, and my shoes standing on top like two giant insects.

I didn't dare move. I called out to him softly. I thought he was watching me from the frame of the half-open door. When I cried out, it seemed like my voice was absorbed by the carpet. Nobody could hear me, I could hear nothing. I waited, immobile. As panic took hold, I was afraid I'd die of a heart attack. There were steps in the corridor, the clinking of porcelain.

'Madam, it is ten o'clock.'

A maid deposited a breakfast tray on the table.

'What are you waiting for? Untie me.'

She looked at me, stunned.

'Sir asked me to wake you. He didn't say that you were tied up.'

She was struggling to obey an order he hadn't given.

'OK, I'll go and get a knife from the kitchen.'

■

The shopkeeper must have given him my mobile number. He called me three days later.

'I tied you up to give you a surprise.'

'Go fuck yourself.'

'Why not?'

I hung up. He harassed me for a whole week. To put a stop to it, one evening I asked my husband to answer for me.

'If you carry on, we will make a complaint against you.'

'Do you know who I am?'

He said his name. My husband apologised.

'She will call you back, I promise.'

'Put her on.'

He followed me into the living room, holding out the telephone like a candlestick.

WE ARRIVED IN MILAN. IN THE STREETS THERE were still little packs of drunks. The shop windows were like light-boxes illuminating the pavements. The station gates were closed. Behind the glass, plunged in shadow, the main concourse was like the scene of a vigil for the dead. I still don't know if the train drivers were on strike, or if in northern Italy they close train stations at night, like churches. I got back in the taxi.

'You should spend the rest of the night in a hotel.'

'With you?'

'I've got some Viagra in the glove compartment.'

'Take me to the airport.'

He started up, laughing quietly at his own boorishness.

I wondered why I'd wanted to take the train. Even a high-speed train is too slow to turn back time. I didn't feel guilty any more. Love stories as often as not end up in a quagmire. They smash into a wall that they have constructed brick by brick. They fall out of the sky like a helicopter that has lost its blades. I had managed to get away, and he had perished.

I had every right to forget those gunshots. He knew very well the click of a revolver being cocked. His hands were not shackled, he could have disarmed me with a single punch. Through cowardice, he had let himself be killed. He knew that one day I would publish the photos I had taken of him in degrading positions. He was afraid he wouldn't be able to bear the gaze of his humiliated children.

I was not obliged to believe myself. Maybe the cops would find that I had actually invented this story. They would prove the presence of armed men in the room at the moment of the murder. They had executed him with an automatic weapon. They would find the revolver in the lake. Ballistics experts would find me blameless. I had stayed on the terrace sulking. I had fled on hearing the shots. I had slipped down the stairs. I had taken off for fear that they might decide to kill a bothersome witness. They would end up sending me to a clinic where a therapist would sort through my troubled memories.

We arrived at the airport.

'Nine-hundred and ten euros.'

I handed him the Amex card. I signed the receipt.

'You seem a bit under the weather.'

'I need to put on my make-up.'

'Good luck.'

The lights in the terminal were indiscreet. They lit up all the faces as if trying to probe the depths of the pupils, the mouths, the wrinkles. It was three o'clock in the morning. The first plane for Sydney would take off at five o'clock. I bought a ticket at the British Airways counter.

'Window or aisle?'

'I don't care.'

'Gate D21. Have a great flight.'

I tossed my bag onto the conveyor belt. The metal detector made a beep. I removed my watch.

The passengers drowsed in the departure lounge. Two young people lay asleep spread out on the seats.

He had made me happy that morning in July when he came to pick me up from the departure lounge where I was preparing to take the plane to France. His grey alpaca suit made his blue eyes all the more intense. I suspected that under his arm was his Smith & Wesson, in the black lizard-skin holster I had given him for Valentine's Day.

I showered him in gifts bought with my husband's money. He had given me, in all his life, only the revolver, and a shantung sweater with sleeves that were too short, although in winter I did sleep in it just to feel enrobed in a second skin paid for with his dough. He told me later that he had taken it from a batch of clothes destined for the employees' Christmas tree at his Dutch subsidiary.

He had obtained from a minister a permit to carry arms, which even allowed him to pass through airport security. When I saw him walk towards me, I felt loved. He would not have pulled a gun on me, he had never threatened or beaten me without my consent. I had total trust in him when I agreed to be tied up. When he cut the ropes with his hunting knife, he placed a hand over my skin to be sure not to cut me. He lapped up the semen that had run onto my breasts, my neck, my smile. He gently massaged away the marks left by the rope, he kissed the stripes left by the whip.

If he had wanted it, I would have been his absolute submissive. I got no pleasure at all from playing the mistress. But men like to be bound and hit by wicked stepmothers from fairy tales.

When I gave him the suit, I knew he would love it, a supple dungeon where the victim is more confined than a foetus in the prison of the uterus. This new practice bound me more than ties of hemp or steel, more than all the chains in the dungeon. One day he would have no alternative but to marry me, to hand himself over to the woman who for so long had got him by the balls. As men put it.

■

He came towards me in a straight line, beating a path through passengers burdened with bags, as if they were weeds. His smile was white, like fangs. He lifted me off the ground. He took me in his arms like a girl given as the victor's spoils by the losing side in a war. At that moment, I was worth more to him than the sea of dollars he had bathed in since childhood. He jetted me off in his jet.

We landed in New York. His penthouse on the roof of Jefferson Tower overlooked Central Park. The only time in our whole story that we spent a fortnight together. He took only a few calls. He cancelled meetings one after another. The suit was not in our luggage. We made love.

He asked his French chef to take a holiday. He made me fried eggs with broken yolks. He served me lobster bisque barely warm from the microwave. He even took to making pancakes, which he managed to burn in the frying pan. We would dip them in a pot of honey to mask the bitterness.

The happiness of being fed by your man. Two air-conditioned weeks looking at a city overcome by sun. Two weeks where we got to know the sweet taste of the reassuring routine of a couple's life, one dreamed of by lovers made weary from fleeting rendezvous and shortened nights. Two weeks when he invented happiness for us.

Like snorting a line of cocaine, tonight in my cell I think of New York.

THE PLANE WAS ALMOST EMPTY. TAKE-OFF IN THE blue night that precedes the dawn. No clouds.

I had not fastened my seat belt. I hoped that a jolt would launch me into the ceiling of the cabin. A head crushed by carelessness. A death useful to everybody. I would survive him by only a few hours. His family would perhaps have agreed that our coffins appear next to one another in a funeral home. A final pathetic meeting they would afford us before taking him away for a mogul's funeral. At least by chance our funeral convoys might cross paths for a moment at a junction, stopping at the same red light before carrying on.

My husband would have me incinerated, with my sister as the only mourner. He would never manage to seize the million dollars, but his financial situation would improve as time went on since I would be gone. Each beat of my heart cost him. I was a luxury beyond his means, a mare whose oats and stabling he paid so another could ride in his place.

'I'm your walking chequebook.'

'Do you want me to leave you?'

'I was joking.'

He tried to laugh to apologise. A fake laugh that made him cough. I gave him a pat on the back. He must have sensed my pity for him, a sentiment far from the love that satisfied him.

A death sent by providence, dazzling, saving me the trouble of committing suicide to prove that I had killed for the simple pleasure of being able to join him. I had heard tell of romantic marriages where, stretched out on a bed, the bride and groom agree to put a bullet in each other. I would have preferred a wedding dress. But then you'd find someone claiming that, in today's fairy tales, princes of finance marry their whores. He couldn't stand anyone else insulting me.

I hadn't killed him. I had invented this memory to scare myself. I needed to refuse to believe in reality. Reality is multiple like a litter of puppies. You must choose your own, and avoid being seduced by the sham of truth. It has never been proven to be anything more than another lie.

The sun rose as the air hostess passed with her trolley.

'Tea or coffee?'

'Champagne.'

'It's a breakfast.'

'I'm not hungry.'

She smiled, and placed the tray on my table anyway. 'On this flight, alcoholic drinks are extra.'

I got the Amex card out of my bag. I brandished it like a referee on a football field showing a yellow card. She came back from the rear of the aircraft with a little bottle of Moët et Chandon.

That morning, even my anxiety cost him. I was thirsty for champagne and hungry for Lexomil. He had paid for the pills, and would pay for the bottles.

I felt better. I changed seats so I could watch the sky through the window. When we travelled, he would sometimes take the controls of the jet the moment it reached its cruising altitude. He didn't know how to take-off, or to land. He'd taken pilot training on a flight simulator. He said that he knew as much as the terrorists who had flown Boeings into the World Trade Center. The pilot seemed relieved when he was allowed to return to his seat.

There was a bedroom at the rear of the aircraft. A large bed where during transatlantic flights we would take long siestas. The noise of the engines would cover up the sound of the lashes I gave him for his pleasure. The next day he would chair a board meeting with stripes down his back.

In his fantasies, he often changed sex. While being whipped, he would murmur that he was my little woman, my little bitch. He wanted me to penetrate him, ferociously, savagely. With the bestiality of the rapists that he imagined in his dreams. He liked objects that ripped, leaving bloody sheets. The chambermaids at the Hilton Palace in New Delhi must remember that. Objects were palliative. Objects were not enough for him.

I WOULDN'T ADVISE ANYBODY EVER TO HAVE MY childhood. Even a murderess doesn't deserve that. My father had a penis, and I saw it often. He had removed the curtains from the glass doors of his bedroom. But he left both panels open, just to be sure.

My mother was rarely in the bed, he preferred to sleep with other females. I hid in a dark corner where I wouldn't need to cover my eyes. I pushed a finger into each ear so I wouldn't hear anything. I hummed to drown it out when his shouts became too loud. Between rounds, he would search the house with his penis out. He'd find me deep in a cupboard, or on the kitchen balcony, or in the old abandoned fridge at the bottom of the garden.

'Come on, you idiot. If the neighbour sees me naked, she'll make a fuss.'

He slapped me, he gave me a kick to hurry me along. He brought me into the bedroom like a video camera that would store the episode in its memory until it was recycled. He positioned me a few steps from the bed. He told me to come nearer when he needed a close-up.

The women rarely got dressed. The more prudish ones pretended not to see me. They ignored me as if I were an out-of-service machine. The others were aroused. I saw the tips of their nipples get hard the moment I appeared. I remember a very white girl, with black hair, who asked me to revive my father's erection.

'Do you want to get me in trouble with the cops?'

'She won't say anything.'

'You've made her cry.'

I ran to the square. I put my head in the sandpit like an ostrich, as they told us at school.

My sister was one year older than me. She didn't interest him. I envied her for being ugly.

When she came home from work, my mother would make the bed in silence. My father still left. I never saw him again. The day after my arrest, he sold an interview to an English tabloid for five hundred euros. He didn't reveal anything worthy of the front page, and it was relegated to page seven between an article on tourism in Ireland and an advert for an anti-ageing cream.

My mother had never found life pleasant. She started to criticise it vehemently after my father left. She blamed us for being born. We were Dad's bad idea.

'You hurt me when you were born. And now, here you are.'

The textile mill where she worked as an accountant closed down. She didn't look for work. She withdrew into the house as if we were at war. The shutters stayed closed day and night. She didn't let us go outside. We were taken out of school. She told us we didn't deserve to go to school.

I remember dark months. The region was rainy, and on the rare days when it was sunny she shut us in our rooms. She had stuck black paper on our windows, to keep the sun out.

Money was tight. She bought items on promotion and filled the fridge with them. For several weeks, she stuffed us with chocolate eclairs. We were sick, we couldn't eat anything. She came back one day with a supply of coffee eclairs. One morning, she turned on all the taps of the gas cooker. She stationed herself in front of the door with her arms outstretched.

'All three of us are going to die.'

We fought her. My sister managed to escape. She roused the neighbourhood. People came. They turned off the gas and aired the place. She calmed down, she thanked them. We were placed with a foster family. An uncle and aunt we had never met came to get us and took us to their home. She took us back after she left the psychiatric hospital. Five years later, she had me committed there for having run off with a married man.

'Doctor, she has a screw loose.'

The uncle and aunt had their doctor intervene to get me released. They protected me. I left them at eighteen to live with a couple.

The woman had approached me at the school gates. She wanted to give me a role in a short film. I lived with them in Lyon. She made love to me. During this, the man would look at our reflection in a mirror that served as the screen of his fantasies. To check that it wasn't falsifying reality, he would glance from time to time in our direction. He called for my help when he was about to come.

They took me to restaurants. They got me drunk on champagne in a nightclub in the Croix-Paquet area. They offered me to men.

An architect found me attractive and put me up in his loft in Paris. I left him for a friend. She had connections. We went to dinners. She gave me lingerie and outfits to please men.

'You need to learn your trade as a woman.'

I discovered partying and the kindly money that falls from the sky. At around eight in the morning, we would come home. I slept in her arms. I woke up in the middle of the afternoon. She squeezed grapefruit for me. She buttered soldiers. She dipped them in eggs she had taken out of the pan, burning her fingers. She put them to my mouth so I would take a bite.

We were happy, I think.

WE HAD A STOPOVER IN MUNICH. ONE OF THOSE landings where the plane jumps. Where it seems to want to come off the runway and immolate the passengers. It came to a peaceful stop at the end of the runway. During the flight, the air hostess had announced a stopover of an hour and forty-five minutes. Before they opened the doors, she apologised on behalf of the airline, saying they definitely anticipated a take-off for Sydney two and a half hours later.

I held on to the handrail as I got off the plane. I staggered along the tarmac to the bus. I was drunk, I felt blurry. The outside lacked contours. Inside, I collapsed without seeing myself.

In the airport terminal, I had begun to make out the white lines on the floor tiles. I walked on them like a tightrope walker, my bag held tight in my arms. People came and went in the chaos, as if they wanted to scribble on the ground with their feet. The million dollars was smiley, it had a nice face, the bright eyes of a child happy to be born. I loved it as the only baby we could have. A baby that he gave me by dint of insistence, caresses, and eternal promises of love. A baby whose custody he denied me.

I sat down on a luggage trolley. I didn't like all the tourists in shorts, off on holiday. An airport employee signalled for me to get up. He tried to explain in German that a trolley becomes dangerous when used as a chair.

I went into a newsagent's. No paper mentioned the discovery of a lifeless man in a latex suit. Until he was found, his death would remain only hypothetical. I should have emptied the little pool on the terrace. Burned him on a bonfire of furniture and Fragonard. I should have watched the murder go up in smoke into the sky.

I sat at a brasserie table. I drank a few coffees. The effects of the champagne and the pills were starting to wear off. It was ten-thirty. I called the bank manager. His assistant told me he was in a meeting.

'Call back in the afternoon.'

'I have to speak to him. My lawyer is going to start proceedings against you.'

'I will see if he can be disturbed.'

He came on the line after five minutes of music that cut off and started again every few measures.

'How can I help?'

'This sequestration is illegal. My lawyer is taking action against you.'

'Tell him to call me.'

'I want you to know the consequences you might face.'

'Send me a fax.'

'I'm travelling.'

He hung up. I called back. The assistant gave me the fax number.

'We need something in writing.'

I went back to the newsagent's. I bought a pad of notepaper. I can't remember what I wrote. The investigating judge later requested a copy. At the trial, the prosecutor circulated it among the members of the jury.

'As you can see, this document is illegible. All that one can observe is that it was written in rage.'

The family's lawyer used this exchange with the bank to argue that I was cold and calculating, and without remorse. Love stories are private planets, and they vaporise when their inhabitants have left. They follow laws that are unknown to the rest of the universe. Unknown, even to those who live there. I am a survivor of a planet erased from the galaxy by an explosion. People judge me according to laws that were not ours at the moment of the crime.

He knew that this time I would pull the trigger. He didn't even let out a cry from the other side of the hood. He wanted me to relieve him of an existence of which he was ashamed. A month earlier, he had sent me a strange email.

'I am a reprobate.'

Despite all the years, he remained a puritan at heart, marked by a strict upbringing. He sought the definitive and purifying punishment that only a violent death could bring. He feared too the barbarism of those who were after him, and he chose me. He was expecting the bullet, he wanted it. He had confiscated my money to force me to kill him. I obeyed him. The million dollars was the gold statue that the ailing emperor gives the samurai who agrees to deliver him from the agony with the stroke of a sword.

I had only worked once, but housewives don't have a job either. When they are young, their parents keep them. Mine were poor, and men played their part. They would have been generous even without sexual relations. My husband was not exactly miserly in his abstinence. I was a fragile girl, and men protected me as if I were a crystal figurine. Their banknotes were like the straw used to stuff a trunk transporting a precious object.

The woman who squeezed grapefruit for me at breakfast died of a rare illness on my twenty-fourth birthday.

For several months, I had to tear myself away from the people of the night in order to care for her.

I was reduced to answering a job advert. I was a salesgirl for a few weeks in a duty-free shop at Roissy airport. I left home before the break of day. I left the shop at night. I lived under the spotlights. I breathed from air vents. We had half an hour for lunch. The manager wouldn't stand for lateness. When there was a disagreement, she would always side with the customer. I quickly understood that I would never blossom in the world of work.

The antique dealer came to buy cartons of cigarettes. He plucked me from this period of my life that I experienced as a punishment. I felt the same relief that I will no doubt feel when I leave prison. I will be like an animal set free after a long journey.

BEFORE THE PLANE DOORS WERE SHUT, I CALLED my husband. He was surprised that I was going to Sydney.

'You don't know anybody in Sydney.'

He complained about the cost of the taxi. I promised him I would get back my money. He wanted to ambush him at his office.

'I'll smash his face in.'

'You'll make a fool of yourself. Plus he's armed.'

'He owes compensation to both of us.'

'This money has sentimental value for me.'

'For me it's a question of honour.'

'I'll call you back.'

Now the plane was full. I was stuck next to an obese man. He was sweating great droplets that ran down his neck. Before we'd even taken off, his shirt collar was soaking wet. The pilot announced that after a stopover of two hours in Hong Kong, we would land in Sydney the next day at seventeen-thirty local time. I had bought a magnum of champagne. I still had a stash of Lexomil.

'I'm Lionel. Are you going on holiday?'

He wiped the sweat that had formed beads around his mouth with the back of his hand as if he was going to swig me from a bottle.

'Don't you want to tell me your name?'

'Betty.'

'Your name isn't Betty, I can see that.'

I have never been able to lie. Even at my trial, when I got up in tears to speak the truth, I saw that the jury didn't believe me. The foreman's gaze became harder, she took me for a pathetic actress. I have never known how to act, not even my own role. I always seem fake, and yet I am sometimes sincere. Only animals are authentic. People never know exactly what they feel. In their pride, they believe that they are someone they like. But they don't measure up to their idea of themselves.

On the fourth day of my trial the moment came for me to testify. I had fasted in prison, and I weighed thirty-five kilos. I was weak, I sometimes got dizzy. I imagined myself falling into the jury box as if into the disused swimming pool of the hotel at the frontier of the Namib Desert, swarming with vipers.

He had taken me there to hunt oryx and hyenas. He asked the guide to lend me a rifle. I shot rounds that were lost in the dunes. When I shouldered the rifle, he stood beside me and held me tight. I felt his penis get hard when my body was shaken by the recoil.

We slept in a giant tent as vast as a suite. The skins of prey dried in the twilight. Slices of oryx grilled on a campfire. I liked the silence of the desert.

He sometimes woke me in the night. He held his hunting knife in his hand. He told me to sit on him. To put the blade to his throat.

'Tell me that you're going to kill me.'

'I'm going to kill you.'

'Tell me that you will cut off my head and bury it in the sand.'

'I will cut it off, I will bury it in the sand.'

'Will you do it?'

'I promise.'

'Cut my throat.'

I made a sawing motion with the blade. He wanted to feel his skin break. I dipped my finger in the oozing blood. I opened his mouth slightly. A frisson of terror as he recognised the taste of blood on his tongue. And then, he came in long spurts.

My cross-examination began in the afternoon, on a scorching day, in a town trapped between mountains. The windows were open. An apple had been my only lunch. The family's lawyer was asking me questions about my life. The prosecutor was harassing me with unpleasant allegations about our story.

'You often cheated on him.'

'No, not even with my husband.'

He read the statement of a French writer who was claiming he had slept with me.

'That's false.'

'He talks about a sixty-nine.'

'It was fellatio.'

People in the room were laughing. I couldn't bear the picture of a scorned man that they were trying to create. It was only my body. A body can sleep with anybody. A vulva does not have feelings. A penis is not affectionate. A body has never cheated on anybody. Since we met, I have made love only with him. I will never again make love with anyone. I will just appear in their beds. I will let them use me. I will give them my flesh. I will be their utensil. I will lend myself. But I will only ever belong to him.

'I'm his wife.'

'He's dead, and you were not his wife.'

'For me, he's still here.'

'His children do not agree with you.'

I fainted. The hearing was adjourned. When it resumed, I was told I could remain seated.

'I will remain standing out of respect for him.'

Everyone burst out laughing.

■

In the evening, in my cell, I talk to him. I don't believe in ghosts. By killing him, I didn't give him eternal life. But I am the grave where I buried him alive.

WE WERE STILL FLYING OVER GERMANY. THEY were distributing blankets. Mr Obese didn't want his.

'You can have it.'

'Thanks.'

I was cold. I was waiting for him to fall asleep. At least he would stop looking at me. I didn't want him to see me drinking. Now and then he was whispering the first name I had made up earlier.

'Betty. Betty. Betty.'

I found slaps in the face out of date. The last ones were given by outraged women in Hollywood movies of the fifties. Besides, experience has taught me that men often prefer slaps to caresses.

'Betty is like the name of a kiss.'

'You're annoying me. My name isn't Betty.'

He started to laugh. I have never liked people laughing. Humour is a stranger to me. I've never understood jokes at all. Since my childhood I have known that life is a serious matter. To live is an odyssey. You have to know what weapons you have and learn to see the chinks in others' armour. Charm is a strategy. When you are not born in the winners' club, attacking the enemy head-on inevitably results in a crushing defeat.

I was ten years old when I was raped by a distant relative who my mother had approached for financial assistance, which he ultimately refused to give. He had chosen a moment when the house was empty. I didn't want to suffer. To struggle would have made him fierce.

'You're nice.'

I understood that a compliment would soften him up. The rape would almost be a cuddle, like a lovers' embrace.

'I don't want to hurt you.'

I did not resist. It's best to surrender yourself to the dentist who is pulling your tooth. Life hurts less when you accept fate. My mother never got to know about this misadventure.

Mr Obese was tormenting me.

'Give yourself another first name.'

I told him that no one called me by my first name.

'You're funny. Do you want me to call you Miss?'

I wrapped myself inside a blanket. I put the other one over my head like a burka.

■

Burkas excited him. He dreamt of a submissive woman, or of an executioner whose gaze he would see through a grill. A mysterious disturbing character. A form with someone behind. Perhaps an armed man, ready to raise the veil and shoot him with bursts of gunfire.

He didn't attach much importance to people. They were different from one another only by the profits he could extract from them. He was as hard in business as he was in love. Pleasure and money were commodities. He had no intention of sharing them. He would have fought even for scraps.

Human beings were flesh machines to him. You can never be sure of totally possessing a living being. He preferred to make suffering machines of them, like the wild beasts that sometimes turned on him in his nightmares. He stroked their wounds with his foot for a long time before shooting them dead. Had he been able to obtain from the minister a permit to hunt the human species, he would not have hesitated to shoot those who resisted his will. That guy did not refuse him anything. He even provided him with my new mobile number when I had changed it to get away from him.

He put fences around people. He hired guards to keep an eye on them, informers to nip in the bud their escape plans, their hope of a new life.

■

He demanded I mistreat him. It was an order. A preroga-
tive of his absolute power. Of the dominatrix, he had
always been the master. I had chosen the latex suit in
a sex shop in Pigalle, considering it a web and me the
spider. An insect's dream. He used it to realise his ultimate fantasy. By despoiling me, he had condemned me to
become his killer. I obeyed him until the end. His murder
belongs to him as does the rest.

'STILL TWENTY-FOUR HOURS BEFORE WE LAND. You're not going to remain silent all the way to Sydney?'

He lifted the blanket. He has the begging eyes of a sex-starved man. They have always come to me to beg for a caress. If you lend them your hand, they want your mouth. They do not see us, they will never listen to us. The appendage they give us is blind and deaf.

'Let me sleep.'

'At least give me a glass of champagne.'

I had opened the magnum bottle on the sly. I had only one cup that I picked up at a water dispenser before boarding.

'I don't have a glass.'

'I'm going to ask the hostess for one.'

'Then you'll get me caught.'

He put his head back on his seat.

'You're not going on holiday.'

'So what?'

'Me neither.'

'I don't care.'

'You're not talkative.'

I didn't want to speak to anybody any more.

I have talked too much since. I threw words into the void. I tried to be sincere. But no sentence can contain the truth. It floats above it like an oil slick on a wave. Before his death, I lied all the time. I always embellished reality. My lies pleased me. I offered them as sweets. When they were sucked, I offered others. At the police station, every time I was summoned, the cops threw them in my face. I ended up growing tired. I confessed.

They would have been better off believing my lies. An assassination would have been better for him, ordered by a holding company under the heel of an Eastern country's dictator. The killers would have brought the latex suit. They would have put it on him under duress. The secret services like to stage executions so the public take heed. The press would have liked this fable, and the public would have been delighted by it as if it were a spoonful of beluga caviar.

The truth is devastating. It is blind. Without mercy. It humiliated his family. It tarnished the image of the father in the hearts of his children. It knocked down the partition separating their room from the cubbyhole where he ran after his orgasms. His children did not deserve the fate that mine inflicted on me. They could have done without this trial. Their mother had over-protected them from the day after the tragedy. She had hired a psychologist for each of them, who helped them step by step through their mourning. The inheritance completed their reconstruction. But then when they testified in court, they were forced to delve into their memories like in a cellar.

The police could have put his body in his Bentley, pushed it off a bridge, and declared that he had died in an accident. But they were unlucky, and the trial brought disgrace on them for a second time.

This truth threw to the media the sordid ending of a debauchee, as though someone's character could be inferred from the circumstances of his death. His sexual life unfolded in the newspapers like the script of a porn movie. My refusal to lie only benefitted voyeurs, timorous people who used his example to take the plunge, embittered people of all kinds who were jealous of his talent as an alchemist who could turn the muddy debts of bankrupts into gold.

When it harms, truth is another crime. Now, I regret that I told it.

Lexomil goes really well with champagne. The murder was travelling inside me, gliding like a gondola. The doll was flying off. A pink oblong balloon, and he would have been the helium. Revolver in hand, I was flying up into the sky. Life was a hunting party. A funfair where bodies were floating like ping-pong balls on little fountains.

■

Mr Obese woke me up. I'm not sure I was asleep. Anyway, the intoxication had disappeared. He opened my table and put my meal tray on it.

'Not hungry.'

'But I can't give it back to the hostess.'

'Eat it.'

He put it on his knees. He attacked his in a state of panic, before the other could get cold.

We were flying over Russia. He often went to Moscow. Sometimes he took me with him. He booked a suite at the Metropol. He woke up at six in the morning. His assistant joined him at seven. I heard them having breakfast in the sitting room. She looked like me, with a perfect body but with a face on top of it not pretty enough to have any hope of ever becoming a super-model. A slightly imperfect package, the kind that does not intimidate men.

They had never been lovers. Other members of his staff took care of certain services when he found himself alone, titillated and stiff behind his desk after he had humiliated a colleague. He was assisted even with mas-turbation. He told me once that he was not a manual worker. He assigned such tasks to his domestics, and I was one of them, like the flunkies in his company.

■

I didn't see him until the evening. I would spend the afternoon hunting in the lobbies of luxury hotels, looking for girls. I took pictures of the candidates. I forwarded them to his mobile. He would reply affirmative, negative, as if I was his recruiting officer. I had to discuss their fees, to pay them an advance in cash, and to demand a receipt so that he could put their services on expenses. I used a receipt pad and they just had to add their names and sign.

'I'm not a translator.'

'No, but in France you can't put whores' salaries through as expenses.'

I couldn't let them escape with the money I had given them. I stayed with them until evening, like a chaperone. In bad English, as they drank vodka, they told me about their lives. Lives, each one like the other. If I erased the snow and the white nights of June, I could confuse them with the life I had lived until our encounter.

Around eight o'clock, I would take them to the Metropol in the limo rented by his company for the occasion. There were too many of them to fit in a taxi. They followed me in single file through the corridors of the hotel. They were all just eighteen, and if their outfits had been more austere, I could have been mistaken for the headmistress of a boarding school.

For him, that was a persistent fantasy: having at his disposal a brood of schoolgirls with pleated skirts. I would bring some in my luggage. I ironed them myself when I arrived, to avoid arousing the suspicions of the chambermaid.

I was ordered to shower the girls like babies before his arrival, and to spray them with my eau de toilette. He wanted us all to emit the same smell. Fine, there are people who can only bear the scent of roses. He would send me an SMS to inform me that he was getting into the lift. I had already arranged the chairs in a square. We were sitting, our hair in pigtails tied with ribbons, our hands flat on our skirts like well-behaved children.

They were afraid of the cudgel he threatened them with, and of the accessories he told them their organs would swallow. I had to reassure them, to stop them running away in their pleated skirts. But in the end, they were left untouched when I let them go at around two o'clock in the morning. His penis had not even been in contact with them.

A girl orgy. After these preliminaries with the bogey-man, I would order them to undress slowly and, one after the other, to join me on the bed where we mixed together bit by bit like the ingredients of a fruit salad. I had to suppress their fits of giggles. Sitting in an armchair, he watched us, trousers around his ankles. With an absent-minded gesture, he would sometimes dust his jacket and check the knot of his tie.

After they left, I slapped him. He submitted to penetration with the cudgel. Then I would kneel in front of him. My duty done, he collapsed in the armchair. Throwing back his head, his jaws half open, his long dangling arms brushing the floor.

When he joined me in bed, he would always ask me if I had brushed my teeth.

Two months after our first night, he gave me the address of a gynaecologist where I could get an HIV test.

'I'll see my general practitioner.'

'No.'

He only trusted him. For more than twenty years, he had sent all his mistresses to him.

Germs frightened him, and viruses made him paranoid. He always disinfected his glans with spirit after each coitus. I was hurt that he would treat my mouth and my anus as cesspits, simmering breeding grounds, tough enough to get through the barrier of a condom. After our sessions, I had to rub the latex suit with an antiseptic solution. I bought bottles of it by the dozen. Bodies were bacteriological bombs to him, and he was as wary of them as he was of parcel bombs.

The gynaecologist's office was located near the Champs-Elysées. A greying and paunchy man, wearing rectangular glasses like two screens. He is often invited on programmes about weight gain during menopause and the prevention of cervical cancer.

Two hundred euros per consultation. He sent me to the Albert Fournier Institute. I had a complete battery of serological tests and punctures, looking for syphilis, chlamydia, gonorrhoea, genital warts and hepatitis. He insisted on giving the results in person. I had to pay again.

'Good news, you have nothing.'

He smiled ironically.

'You're fit for service.'

I believe I was a brave little soldier. I obeyed, to the point of considering the least of his fancies as one of my most precious desires. I would have agreed to be his shield to protect him from a random bullet. His murder was the consequence of my excessive love. I killed him from loving him too much. I'd rather have this long stay in jail than the tragedy of our paths never having crossed.

RUSSIA WAS UNFOLDING INTERMINABLY. A COUNTRY whose oil wells and gas deposits he dreamt of colonising. Before buying places, he acquired people. Mercedes 500s, hectolitres of Sauternes, and for their mistresses, solitaires purchased on place Vendome ... although I never had the right to these. But he had enemies at the head of the State. Tsars too rich to let themselves be corrupted. Ex-KGB tsars to whom he was worth no more than the magazine of a Kalashnikov. He was on respite. He would be dead by now anyway.

He owned Kalashnikovs. In his Val de Loire chateau, there were huge cellars, vaulted wine stores where grands crus were waiting peacefully for their jubilees, unless they were given away before they became centenarian and, impressed by their great age, no one would dare to drink them. He who was afraid of alcohol and hated wine.

He had concreted a part of the cellar. An eight-square-metre room, furnished with shelves and armour-plated cupboards. It was lit by halogen lamps protected by Plexiglas boxes. The unexpected explosion of a light bulb would have blown everything to pieces. The chateau would have been pulverised, they would have found bits scattered as far as Blois.

An arsenal holding thousands of handguns, rifles, machine guns, defensive grenades and a stock of munitions that, according to him, would have been enough to execute ten thousand people.

'On condition you shoot straight.'

'You shoot straight.'

'With the explosives, you can even massacre twenty thousand people if they are in a crowd.'

Six months before his death, he had even acquired a heavy machine gun, a rocket launcher and a crate of landmines whose effects he had tested in a remote corner of the park, on a fox terrier that he had bought for the purpose at a kennels in Romorantin.

'He wasn't completely dead.'

'Did you finish him off?'

'With a shovel, I hadn't my gun with me.'

Arms legally bought, and the duplicate of the bill sent to his insurer. A fortune is a power more solid than the power of presidents, who periodically prostrate themselves before the people to beg for an ephemeral crown.

■

Sometimes we would stay there all afternoon. He liked to dismantle guns, to lubricate them. He rubbed the barrels with a chamois and polished the wooden butts like furniture. I helped him to buff them with a woollen cloth. He would tilt them in the light to see them gleam. He had the smile of a child at play. A smile reserved for revolvers, firearms, all the toys of his Ali Baba's cave.

'When you have guns, you have to look after them.'

One day in January 2003, he slipped a revolver into my hand.

'Feel, how cold it is.'

He was caressing it with his fingertips like a white mouse.

'A funny animal.'

'Yes.'

'Would you like to adopt one?'

He caressed my forehead with the same tenderness he had shown to the revolver.

'Would you?'

I never said no to him.

'I'd like to.'

'Keep it, it's for you.'

I gripped it between my fingers. I put it flat against my heart. I kissed it. This kiss excited him, as if I had given it to a call girl he had asked me to rent to satisfy his desire to see me sleep with a woman.

He had an erection. He opened out a camp bed. The kind of bed soldiers sleep in during wars. He placed it in the middle of the room. We made love. Surrounded by guns, he was tender. It was as if they were watching over him. He took me. I came.

There was a shooting gallery at the end of the cellar, with targets in human shapes. Sometimes he would stick up a picture of Putin, or of a director from one of his subsidiary companies who was about to be sacked. He taught me how to use the revolver.

'You're gifted.'

My hand did not shake. I could empty the cylinder in bursts and make a tight group. He enjoyed frightening himself. Sometimes he would stand at the bottom of the tunnel, pressed against the wall, and tell me to shoot.

'Do it as if I'm not here.'

'I can't.'

'Go on.'

I obeyed. Bullets whistled past his ears. I saw his arm rising bit by bit, but eventually he would resist the temptation to catch them with his hand.

'Reload.'

'No.'

'Yes.'

I would start again and again. I was overcome by fatigue. My shoulder muscles started to ache. My shots were less precise; some bullets strayed to the edges of the target.

'Take care.'

I put the revolver on the floor.

'I can't stand up any more.'

'Try to relax.'

He showed me how to relax. He bent the top of his body forward and let his arms dangle.

'Breathe, blow. Move up slowly, breathing through your nose.'

I aimed again, I shot.

Every time he took me to the cellar, he inflicted this game on me again. When he reversed the roles, he tied my hands and my feet. Sometimes he pretended he was aiming at me. He waited for me to start screaming.

'You can yell, no one will hear you.'

He spared me, and emptied his magazine into Putin's face. One eye and half a forehead were missing.

'Stop crying, it's over.'

He came towards me with a smile. He carried me on his back as you'd carry an injured man on a battlefield. He lay me on the floor. When he regained his composure he would reload the Colt and take out his hard member. He aimed at my head, and at the last minute would shoot one of the sandbags which he had positioned as a barricade, as though he were afraid of an ambush. Sometimes his sperm would gush out. His tense face would become pained, as if he had been shot dead.

He came round. He cut off my straps. He became sweet suddenly. A cruel child rejected by the army. A dream of adventures in the dirty waters of harbours. Becoming a combat diver, sticking bombs under aircraft carriers. Having the chance to die a hero. He was declared unfit for service because of psychiatric disorders. He confided in me one panicky evening, in one go, using phrases that seemed stuck together so that the pain of telling them would not last as long. Then, he ran to the bathroom. I joined him. He was in the shower, sobbing.

'I'm not crying, it's the water.'

I went back quietly to the room to let him think that I believed him.

Despite the fear that he could kill me, and dispose of my corpse in the dungeon of the castle, whose dark well he had shown me once, with its smell of dead animals, its staircase with collapsing steps, and streams of black water that I had taken for trickles of blood. The terror that he would erase me little by little from his mind. He had enough willpower to vitrify my souvenir and to wipe it from the map of his memory.

The dread of seeing him emerge at the last minute in front of the target, of seeing him hit right in the heart by one of my shots, and of staying there gripping his corpse forever without daring to reappear upstairs, waiting to be arrested or to starve to death.

Yet nothing had ever managed to spoil my pleasure. In this cellar, we were alone, together. I lost myself, I had hope. I even allowed myself the joy of believing that he belonged to me.

THE PLANE WAS FLYING OVER CHINA. MY NEIGH-
bour was not sweating any more. He was sleeping, lips
tight, face pale and dry, his hands curved as if he were
afraid that a cup of coffee knocked over by the air hostess
might scald his testicles.

I stepped over him. I knocked against him. He moved,
but his sleep held firm. I fell in the middle of the aisle.
The lights were off, only two or three small lamps were
throwing beams on the insomniacs' seats. I got back up.
I walked as far as the toilet. I threw up in the bowl. I
looked at myself in the mirror. I could have done without
this face. Dark circles don't suit me. I have always chosen
light-coloured eyeshadow, smoky eyes make me ugly. I
had taken the time to put on make-up after the murder.
That was already yesterday. I had even added a bit of
pink on my lips before starting the car.

All those kilograms lost in six months. Without men-
tioning the ones I would lose in jail. He had worn me
down. A pebble that has rolled too much. A man like a
storm. A girl broken into pieces. A girl already born in
poor condition. Falling on the delivery table as a sign

of bad luck. I made an effort to carry on hoping. It had become a kind of work. I wanted to strengthen my hope like a bicep. At least to keep it in shape, to prevent it from wasting.

Sometimes, I had the instinct of an animal. I was trying to run away, like horses leave a plain at a gallop before an earthquake. He was capturing me, he preferred the catastrophe to my absence.

From the first weeks, he had wanted to know about our future. He told me jokingly that a friend of a friend, a magus, would give us a glimpse of our destiny. He would hide from us the date of our deaths, he would spare us the tale of the minor pitfalls and the seasonal diseases that we would surely contract during some winters.

'But he will tell us if it's worth it.'

'If what's worth it?'

'Investing ourselves in a love story.'

One evening, he arranged a meeting at an old restaurant in rue Vivienne, near the Palais Royal. I waited for him for forty-five minutes. I was drinking glasses of champagne, refusing the advances of lonely men, and of those who took advantage of their dates' visits to the toilets to ask me for my phone number.

When he arrived, he rushed in the direction of a guy who was standing at the bar and who had not once turned to look at me. He took him to the table.

'Let me introduce my shrink.'

He had the big head of a dwarf, eyes that were too blue, a mouth with thick dark-red lips.

'A clairvoyant.'

I learnt later that he had seen him every week for thirteen years. Sometimes, he would even take him in his plane for a four-thousand-five-hundred-feet-high consultation. In his accounts, he would appear as an adviser attached to continuing education.

'You're not going to say anything?'

'Hello, sir.'

He touched my hand, and wiped his with a tissue that he took from his pocket, pretending to cough.

'Aren't you going to kiss me?'

I gave him a resounding kiss from afar. He grabbed a waiter, and ordered dinner without asking us what we would have chosen had he shown us the menu. At restaurants, he never asked for my input. When he wanted to punish me, he chose meals that I found disgusting.

'And also a bottle of red wine and a Perrier.'

'We have at the moment an excellent Brouilly.'

'Anything you want, I won't drink it anyway.'

A perfect boor, but I have always had a weakness for brutal men who impose their choices on me. I was often disappointed, because on the whole they later reveal themselves to be indecisive dictators, little marshmallow generals who stick their backsides out to privates to have them booted.

As a starter, we had a fish terrine. The shrink didn't touch his.

'Eat.'

'They put all kinds of things in terrines.'

'It's like the unconscious, full of filth.'

'So you're still indulging your need to order without consulting others.'

'Shut up.'

He pinched my cheek. He seemed satisfied with me. The shrink was offended, like a serf whose baron wants to exchange him for a barrel of herrings.

He turned to him.

'Go on, question her.'

'It would be better to see her at my office.'

'Obey.'

He took a spiral notebook from his pocket.

'Miss, I'd like you to tell me your story.'

'I don't have a story.'

The shrink sighed.

'You don't examine a patient in a public place.'

'Do you really want to pay the bill?'

He caught my bag that I had left on the banquette. He threw it to me like a ball.

'We're leaving. You'll go and see this arsehole in the morning.'

He pulled me. He dragged me to the door. He turned around. He started to shout.

'And don't even think of squeezing money out of her, otherwise you're fired.'

He pushed me outside.

'You didn't want to talk in front of me? Are you hiding something from me?'

'Who do you think I am?'

'A woman.'

I wiped my cheek. I'm not sure he had spat on me. It wasn't raining, but even when the weather is nice a water drop can happen to fall from a cloud that forgets itself.

He got into his Bentley. He scratched a car as he drove off. He disappeared at the corner of the street. I called my husband to tell him I had to stay in France for another week.

'I don't see you any more.'

'I found work as a replacement in a jewellery shop in Montparnasse.'

'It's good that you are starting to work again.'

'I do what I can.'

I spent the following days, melancholic, in my house in Avallon.

He was calling me, and I was ignoring all his calls. He was leaving me insulting messages.

'How much do you cost?'

In others, he was apologising like a child.

'I'm very sorry. I hurt you.'

One morning there was calm. I even thought there was a problem with the phone network. The next day, I received a call from his assistant to inform me that she had just booked an appointment for me with his shrink.

'Tomorrow at 3 p.m. Can I confirm?'

I had never been to a psychoanalyst. But I was sure my psyche was clean enough. My childhood was not a vice. My past, I didn't want it. I was responsible only for the future, where nothing had yet happened. I wanted him to know that. Once he felt reassured, perhaps he would choose to love me. I would be able to leave him with my head held high.

'Are you busy on that day?'

'No.'

I stayed fifteen minutes in his office.

'Don't you have anything else to ask me?'

'Don't worry. I know enough to give him my report.'

'You are going to tell him what?'

'That you're not exactly a lunatic.'

I left satisfied. He had asked me no embarrassing question about my sexual life beginning with a rape. He could have imagined that I had retained a hatred of men. It happened that I slept with women, but I didn't feel lesbian and I didn't consider men as hostile.

In the evening, I took a train to join my husband. He came to pick me up at the station. Only five days had passed since that dinner. He was suspicious.

'You told me that this replacement would last a week.'

'I'm not made for work.'

He became pensive.

'You could become an artist.'

'I don't know anyone who could help me.'

'You've got an antique-dealer friend.'

'Maybe I'm not talented.'

'You don't know that. You've never painted. And anyway, that's not the question. There are bad painters who earn a lot of money.'

He bought me an easel. I discovered that I was talented. I also started to write poems. But I never managed to play a single chord on the guitar we excavated from the attic, the one he played *Forbidden Games* on when he was busking as a student.

The antique dealer refused to help me.

'You have to succeed by yourself. I'm not an art dealer.'

Just before the drama, I was about to publish a book of watercolours. The publisher was insisting that I contribute to the printing costs. My husband was grumbling. He was afraid it wouldn't sell.

'At the moment, I can't afford to invest with no hope of a return.'

AN ETERNAL FLIGHT, AS IF TIME ZONES WERE baulking at letting us go back in time. New meal. I had an empty stomach. I swallowed everything with the last few gulps of champagne at the bottom of the magnum bottle. I was not thinking about the murder any more. I was not even thinking about him.

When I come back from Sydney, I might hole myself up for a few weeks in Avallon. I decorated the house myself. It was too small to have friends at the weekends, but the pleasure of staying in a calm refuge was enough for me. Now I will have to redecorate the bathroom. I was going to paint a fresco above the bath. I had already torn down the old wallpaper and put on the coating.

He had often come there to track me down. He would hide in the woods to watch me with the infrared binoculars that he used for hunting bears. He would see me come and go in the living room and glide, scantily dressed, around the bedroom that I had fixed up in the attic. He was like a predator watching and waiting for the propitious moment to swoop down on its prey.

He always stayed at an inn at the foot of a vineyard, a few kilometres away from my house. Sometimes, he would wait several days before coming and taking me by surprise, managing his business from there, even calling his colleagues for a workshop in the restaurant, which he'd had closed on the pretext of a private reception.

He would eventually storm me. He would wait until all the lights were out. He didn't have a spare key, but there was no shutter on the kitchen window. He would push it, and most of the time the old bolt would yield. Sometimes he broke the window with his elbow. I have the deep sleep of those who drop off only when they are knocked out by pills. I wouldn't hear him entering my room, or undressing and throwing his shoes on the floor. He wouldn't bother to shake me to inform me of his presence, nor would he begin with any lubricating preliminaries. I would wake up screaming, his penis stuck in my dry vulva.

When I went downstairs in the morning, he would be waiting for me with croissants and fresh bread he had bought with money he had pinched from my bag. He wouldn't apologise for his savagery during the night. I would not have understood his apologising.

I enjoyed being his prey, and that he came to take it by surprise at the bottom of its burrow. He was the only man who had wanted me that much.

He would question me while I was drinking my bowl
of coffee.

'Why didn't you reply to my messages?'

'I don't know.'

He beat me tenderly.

I would go back up to Paris with him. We were
stopped from time to time.

'Two hundred and fifty-six kilometres. Please get out
of the vehicle.'

'You're wasting my time.'

He would call a number. Hand his mobile to the cop.

'It's for you.'

The cop would give it back to him with a sigh after
listening to the interlocutor for a few seconds.

'You can go.'

We would set off again. He never wanted to tell me
who it was that got him out of these difficult situations
every time.

'Are you sleeping with the police commissioner?'

He would look at me with the expression of a
little brat.

'They all suck my dough like a dick.'

One evening, in December 2004, we had dinner in the
secret place of a member of the government. A loft at the
back of a courtyard with so little furniture that he had

probably never lived there. A red-haired beanpole opened the door. A delivery man brought sushi while I was drinking lukewarm vodka with her on a sofa that had just been freshly unpacked, its back still covered with plastic. They were talking between themselves at the back of the room, sitting on folding chairs. They were not speaking to us. They ate their sushi directly from the containers.

She wouldn't stop chattering. She was telling me that she had started her career in nude cinema.

'Porn movies?'

'Not at all, in contemporary art movies. Nudity, simply nudity.'

She was going to get her bottom and breasts changed.

'They operate in Madrid next Monday.'

She showed me a picture of Greta Garbo.

'I'd like to be able to afford her face.'

This exorbitant operation would last for seven or eight hours. She asked me why I had not had my nose shortened.

'You think it's too long?'

'It's a hick nose.'

She took a pill box full of cocaine out of her bag.

'At least you can sniff with it.'

There was not even a table. She made lines on the armrest. They came to join us. The statesman squatted down and inhaled rafts of it. Then they went to talk, far from us.

'You're not having any?'

'No.'

I stood up. I finally found the bathroom. My father had always told me that my nose looked like a stone marten's. I sat on the edge of the bath. I was not crying. I was waiting for the evening to pass. I was chewing tablets. I was looking down. I was afraid of the mirror.

As we left, the girl was lying, pale, on the couch. The statesman was furious.

'She can't hold her drink. She'd better have a liver transplant.'

On the doorstep, he wished me luck.

'Why?'

He didn't answer. He turned towards him with a laugh.

'If you get killed, don't count on me coming to the funeral.'

We got lost in the courtyards before finally finding the exit. He was anxious. I saw he was shaking a bit.

'The Republic is going to chuck me on the scrapheap, just like everybody will.'

'I won't chuck you.'

He smiled.

'You'll be my bulletproof vest.'

'Yes.'

He touched my cheek. We were alone in the middle of unlit apartment buildings.

A moment of privacy. The rest of humanity seemed to me to be lying face down on the ground. We were aiming our rifles at them. I was sure I loved him, and our love terrified them like a death threat.

Back home, he wanted me to make vicious love to him.

WE LANDED IN HONG KONG. THEY MADE US DIS-
embark for the plane to be cleaned. In the terminal, Mr
Obese followed me, sweating. His eyes were dirty and his
mouth furry from his nap. I turned around and clapped
my hands as if to get rid of a fly.

'But, what?'

He gawked at me, and rushed towards a fire exit,
whose flashing pictograph attracted him like an SOS. I
would have preferred that a woman had approached me.
I would have felt close to someone. Two women are never
that far from each other. They belong to the same tribe.

I ordered a triple espresso at the counter of a cafeteria. I
sat down at a table occupied by a not-so-pretty girl. She
had long blonde hair that looked like mine. She turned
to face the wall; I didn't dare speak to her. My husband
had left messages on my mobile. He couldn't understand
my confusion. He was still asking me why I was going
to Sydney.

'You're such a child.'

To reassure him, I could have told him that I wanted to see kangaroos jumping over the cars in rush-hour traffic jams.

I stood up. The young woman didn't turn her head to see me leaving. I didn't want to use up my mobile battery. I called him from a phone box. He asked me how much the ticket had cost.

'That's very expensive.'

'I'm in economy class.'

'You shouldn't have gone so far away.'

'I wanted to go far away.'

'But why Australia?'

I asked him to wash the car.

'The interior as well.'

'Is there a problem?'

'If the police ask you, say that I stayed at home last night until midnight.'

'The police?'

I hung up. Later I bore a grudge against him because he forgot to clean the steering wheel. My hands had left powder marks on the leather.

The first call was made for the flight to Sydney. I was going around in circles with the crowd. When it decided to follow a direction, I continued to circle around with the few indecisive people. I was looking at the shops passing before my eyes. Always the same window with ceramic Buddhas and plastic dragons. Behind, newspapers were on display shelves and a TV screen hung on the wall. I was struggling against the centrifugal force not to be propelled into the whirlwind. My name was called.

'Last call before departure.'

I managed to place myself in a flow moving towards the boarding gates. A lazy flow, too dense for me to start running. Hong Kong was as good as Sydney. I would hide here, waiting for the police to arrest the culprits. I saw on the departures board that the flight had just been delayed for thirty minutes. I didn't try to struggle any more.

The hostess made me board.

'We almost took off without you.'

I got back to my place. The magnum bottle had been collected. The plane smelled of air freshener. Mr Obese stood up to let me into my seat. He looked at me for a while, with the eyes of a punished slave. He fell asleep after take-off.

MY SISTER ADVISED ME TO PIERCE CONDOMS
through their wrappers, with a needle. In case he
abstained too long from vaginal penetration, I could
inseminate myself with the tips of my fingers, using the
barely-diluted sperm from my mouth.

He wouldn't have minded. He liked pregnant women.
He asked me to find some on Meetic.com. Most refused,
and the others were expensive.

'The price of a rifle.'

He would caress the stomach. He licked it like an
animal its offspring. After he came, he massaged it as if
with a cream. On two occasions, the women changed
their minds halfway through the session. They threw the
money back in my face and demanded the return of the
expenses form I had made them sign.

His demands were difficult to satisfy. My husband
moaned about it.

'You're really doing a secretary's job.'

'He calls me his sexual secretary.'

He was put out that he didn't pay me a salary. He even phoned him several times, asking him to give me the position of assistant in one of the companies in his group.

'Dirty pimp.'

He hung up on him.

From the beginning, they had a difficult relationship. When my husband came with me for a weekend in his chateau, they sometimes couldn't get along despite all my efforts. He insulted him. He knew everything about him. He'd had him investigated, just like he'd done with me.

'You're not even a doctor.'

He felt humiliated that his diploma didn't give him the title of doctor.

'You're a con man.' It seems he had stolen money from his ex-wife in order to get started, after he'd lived with her for twenty-five years in Uganda.

'An old woman. She could have been your mother.'

He didn't have any choice. His parents were dead. She paid for his studies. When he told her he intended to leave her, she got a marabout to cast a spell on him. He blamed me.

'She's not even your wife.'

We had got married one drunken night in Las Vegas. A contract that had no validity. A few years ago, he wanted to regularise it. I made him realise that we would then have to get divorced, on the understanding that he would marry me afterwards.

'You're right, in that case it would be better to do it straightaway.'

The dinners were painful. He never went anywhere without an entourage. Heads of multinationals, politicians, actresses, and a collection he called his team of dickheads, even if it included a few women. He liked to provoke him in public.

'I hear that you have a prick, so show it off. Give us a laugh.'

He often mocked him about the size of his penis. He saw a photo I had taken of him coming out of the icy water of a river where we had bathed nude one summer's day. It wasn't at its best, and he wanted him to participate in our lovemaking in order to humiliate him. He often even shared with me his desire to penetrate him.

'To put him in his place.'

One afternoon when he got backache during a walk, he asked my husband to manipulate his spine. I had a lot of trouble getting him to agree. At the end of the treatment, he noticed that his erect rod was popping out of his trousers, which he had undone to ease access to the coccyx. My husband later told me off for not having thought to take a photo with my mobile.

'A souvenir.'

I took more compromising snaps than that. I set up an automatic Nikon on a tripod to keep a record of our sexual activities. He didn't mind the presence of the camera. He played with the fear that one day the images would be divulged. The lens stimulated him. A frisson went through him every time the shutter went off. I could feel the grain of the goosebumps where the latex didn't cover his skin.

Back home, I selected a few of them to print.

Three months before the event, anonymous death threats left every night on his voicemail made him suspicious. He even suspected his nearest and dearest of plotting against him. One night when we were having dinner for two in a restaurant on avenue Montaigne, he asked me to give him all the photos.

'And delete the files.'

'Do you distrust me?'

'Yes.'

I wanted to slap him. I held back to deprive him of the pleasure.

'I'm not talking to you.'

I didn't speak to him. He tried to kiss me in the car. I pushed his face away with my whole hand. He drove sheepishly. I slept on the sofa. He came to wake me up in the night. I refused to enact the fantasy he demanded. For a bit of peace, I helped him to come, using a lazy hand. He fell asleep on the floor like a big dog.

He woke me up in the morning before leaving.

'Do you love me?'

I looked at him in silence. I didn't know. I didn't want to lie. He was scared that I would say no.

'Have a good day at work.'

'I love you.'

His eyes were full of terror.

During that period, I used to turn off the television when the news came on. I was afraid I'd hear them announce his assassination. The image of a body in a business suit on the plaza of La Défense. A portrait of him hastily retrieved from the archives, and a brief biography like an epitaph.

He knelt before me.

'Go on, say it.'

I was afraid I'd be filled with remorse if something happened to him.

'I love you.'

When he'd gone, I decided to put the photos in a safe place at my uncle and aunt's house, since he didn't even know they existed. I got dressed and hurried to Gare de

Lyon. I took the train to Avallon, where the prints were stashed under my bed.

I left Avallon at around three o'clock. I had to change trains half way. I arrived at night in their tiny town. Streets, lit up for Christmas, were empty. A bar was still open, and a couple at the counter were nursing beers.

I walked to their house. They always left the garden gate open. I knocked on the window of the living room. They both came to open the door. In their old age, they never moved alone any more.

'You should have told us you were coming, we would have made you *truites au bleu*.'

I gave them the bag of photos sealed with tape.

'Put this in your safety deposit box at the bank.'

'We don't have one.'

'The main thing is, don't tell anyone. If I die, burn the lot in the fireplace.'

'Are you ill? Should we call the doctor?'

'No – I'm very well.'

I went to have a glass of wine in the kitchen. They watched me drink sitting at the table. The waxed orange tablecloth had faded since my childhood.

'We'll make your bed.'

'I can't stay.'

'It's almost midnight.'

I kissed them. They both smelled of the same cologne that I used to smell when I lived with them.

'You're a bit pale, you should get some rest.'

I went upstairs. I turned on the strip-light. I took the cologne. A large square bottle that had always sat proudly on the shelf above the sink. I had never seen it empty. It must have miraculously refilled itself the moment it was sprinkled.

They waited side by side at the bottom of the stairs.

'Can I take this?'

'We'll give you a new one.'

'I prefer this one.'

'We have a supply in the linen cupboard.'

I kissed them.

'I really have to go.'

'And what are you going to do out there in the dark?'

'He's waiting on the square in his Bentley.'

'Tell him to come and have some coffee before getting back on the road.'

A timid invitation. They had never met this man whose face I had once pointed out on the cover of an American magazine. They had never seriously imagined he would ever touch his lips to one of their earthen-ware cups.

'Don't worry, we'll rent a safety deposit box.'

'I'll come back to see you soon.'

'See you soon.'

▪

The only hotel was in darkness. I rang the bell, I knocked on the door. The night watchman was on holiday, or there wasn't one at all. I walked to the station. They had put on the night lights. I slept on a bench next to the sandwich machine.

An employee woke me up at six in the morning.

'I was afraid you'd died of cold.'

'I'm numb.'

I came back to Avallon with bronchitis. I slept for three days. I turned off my mobile. In a dream, I was walking barefoot in a stream of messages croaking like frogs.

STUPEFIED BY THE LONG VOYAGE, THE PASSENGERS slept despite the sun streaming through the windows. I tried to stay awake. I fought against the effects of the champagne I ordered little by little from the air hostess. I didn't want to succumb to sleep, only to wake up in panic during landing. I planned to set myself up for life in Sydney. I would subscribe to a merciful religion to feel less guilty for having lived. I had been born in the wrong hemisphere. Perhaps serenity awaited me in Australia.

The family will be relieved that I accept the million dollars in the final settlement. In exchange, I will send a letter waiving any claim against his estate. I could have released a message recorded on my home answerphone. He swore to marry me, on the life of his children and on the one we would soon be having together. Armed with such evidence, it would not have been absurd to assert rights to his estate.

Perhaps I had been inseminated the day of the murder. When he grasped that I would agree to the session, he had ejaculated. A quick stream running down his flannel trousers. A stealthy slide of my hand, and then I put it in my vagina so the semen wouldn't be wasted.

On arrival, I would check into a hotel. I was ready to lie flat to give the foetus every chance of getting through the first weeks without incident. I had read that for the first twenty-five days, the slightest shock could be fatal to the embryo.

Once the child is born, his corpse will be exhumed. DNA will confirm him as his legitimate heir. The family would have to send me maintenance payments for the cost of his upbringing.

Sometimes I put a nappy on his father. While changing our child, I won't be able to avoid thinking of him. I will be sad that he hadn't known him. But his absence will spare our child the suffering he endured at the hands of his own progenitor.

'We have no alcohol left.'

The air hostess thought I was drunk. I gave up. Anyway, I wasn't feeling well. Every time I closed my eyes, I was falling into the void.

He sometimes told me off for drinking too much. We spent a week's holiday with his children at his chateau. He had invited a friend, and I was supposed to be his wife. I envied his ex-wife, who would turn up with him years after their divorce for charity dinners that she organised in aid of leukaemia research – her niece had died of it when she was sixteen. I suspected they still slept together when he spent Christmas with her in Brighton. I tried to stupefy myself with Bourgogne to forget that he didn't grant me the status of a favourite, the recognition women dreamed of in the court of Louis XV. If at that time he wanted to hide our relationship from his children, he was also proud to show them off to me. He said that they looked like him.

'Don't you think?'

'Ours will look even more like you.'

'We'll see.'

'He will be your favourite child.'

'Shut up.'

'He will be handsome, you'll lose all interest in the others.'

'Stop shouting.'

I pounded him in the chest. I bit his hand, which he had put over my mouth to keep me quiet.

'He will be your masterpiece.'

I was swaying, I let myself fall on the floor in the library, the location of our secret meetings. He took me up to my room, trying to make no noise. He lay me on the bed. He smacked me to bring me round.

One evening, I didn't react to the slaps. He tried to listen to my heartbeat, he heard nothing. The doctor came, he diagnosed an alcoholic coma. The next day, I had bruises on my cheeks. He sent me back to my husband in an ambulance so nobody else would see them.

His son turned eighteen in September 2004. He forced him to join him in Paris for the All Saints' Day holidays, and whilst my husband pretended to believe I was in Avallon, I spent whole weeks with him.

'I want you to learn a bit how to run the shop.'

He had to go with him to his office. He attended certain meetings, he followed him on his travels. His instructions were to watch, to listen, to keep his mouth shut.

'You will be invisible.'

His colleagues were not even allowed to say hello to him. His assistant gave the order to visitors not to pay more attention to the young man sitting in the chair than to a broom left behind by a cleaner. He boasted that he had fired a man from accounts who had apologised for bumping into him getting out of the lift.

The kid went back home traumatised from having had to play the role of a ghost all day. In the early evening, we were often alone. His father rarely left the office before nine or ten o' clock. I opened a bottle of champagne to help him chase away the blues.

'I prefer apple juice.'

'At least have one glass.'

'OK – half and half.'

He drank the mixture gladly. I could make him laugh by tickling him. For my amusement, he would imitate his father and his way of hissing his s's like a snake. I had never thought that such complicity was possible with this child who I had for a long time considered a rival to the one who would be born one day from our union. I began to see him as the stepson that he would become after our marriage.

My memory is of a fragile boy. When he had drunk too much, he lay on the couch and put his head on my knees. I caressed it and, closing his eyes, he would smile as he dozed off. One evening we both fell asleep.

His father found us like that. A cold anger, an icy anger. Without a single word, he took his gun out of its holster. He aimed at me. The bullet went through the upholstery of the couch. It smashed a lamp-stand before shattering a window and disappearing over the rooftops of the avenue Raymond Poincaré. The next day at seven, a driver came to get his son. He dropped him off at Le Bourget airport, where the jet was waiting to take him back to his mother.

■

I never bore him a grudge over that shot. Instead of throwing me out, he immediately took me into the bedroom. We had never made love so peacefully. We could hardly hear his son crying at the far end of the apartment.

Maybe imaginary crying. He slept on a little bed that he had installed in the far-flung projection room where we would shut ourselves away from time to time to watch epics or old westerns. It was soundproofed, and he preferred to know that he was there, far from the noise of our grappling.

In the end I managed to convince him that the position we were in was tender and chaste. He must have mistaken a fold in his son's trousers for an erection.

'Even you, you didn't believe that.'

He would have killed me. The target was too close for him to miss. The shot was in anger, like smacking the hand of a child whose antics have made you angry.

His son didn't reply to any of the letters I sent him from prison. I would have liked to hear him tell the court what he saw on the twenty-second of December 2004. That evening, he told me about it, still deathly pale.

'I shouldn't have looked.'

His father had left him alone in his office while he inflicted a terrible quarter-of-an-hour on his assistant to relieve his morning stress. He couldn't resist the temptation of going through his inbox. He saw a few business messages. Then he found a message without a subject that had arrived at night. His account had been hacked – the message looked like it had been sent from his own address. There were three photo attachments.

In the first, he saw him bound naked on a metal bench. In the second, he was howling, with his penis in flames. The third picture showed his body sliced up on a kitchen table. A swollen, blackened head, eyelids closed, a toothless mouth with the lips torn off. His limbs and his torso in three slices were arranged in the form of a star.

I gave the kid a glass of champagne saturated with several anti-anxiety drugs, and I sent him to bed. He slept for twenty-four hours.

Instead of going home, he called me that night at ten o' clock to arrange to meet in a café on the avenue de la République. A neighbourhood that to my knowledge he was not in the habit of frequenting. He was in a strangely good mood.

'I've decided we should stay in a hotel.'

'What hotel?'

'A knocking-shop in Barbès. You will bring up a whore to help us out. Or a bloke, a black man, two black men, three black men.'

He started laughing. A laugh that shouted. People turned their heads.

'You should have warned me. I would have chosen them this afternoon. I would have brought them to your place.'

'This will be more discreet.'

'Still, it would be better at home.'

Even when his son wasn't there, I always made the studs use the back stairs. He used men more and more because they brought a certain virility.

A journalist threatened in 2003 to make an allusion in a gossip magazine to his penchant. He feared this revelation would make him look like a homosexual, although he claimed only ever to have loved women. In the end, the article didn't come out. He hired the guy as a communications consultant. This fictional and salaried post inspired gratitude, and the offer to spread rumours about personalities whose abasement could be useful to him.

He had left his Bentley at the office.

'We're going there incognito.'

He had brought his scooter. An old vehicle with rusted chrome, with a lock he never used. He parked on rue Myrha in front of a hotel with dirty windows. A narrow entrance, under a bare light bulb a counter, and behind it a lady wearing a Muslim veil. He gave a hand signal, and without saying a word she gave him the key. We clambered up a flight of stairs in darkness. The corridor was just as dark. The yellow light from a spotlight hanging by its wires. He opened the door of room eight.

'We'll act like we're camping.'

'It looks like an immigrant's room.'

The ceiling was low, and was missing some plaster. A little window, with cracked panes. A quivering wooden bed with a mattress as thin as a chair cushion. A sink behind a screen.

'Is that the bathroom?'

'The toilets are on the second floor.'

He seemed pleased with himself. At the same time, I could see the agitation in his fingers, which he nervously stacked on top of one another.

'You'll take a shower tomorrow morning when you get home.'

'Are there vermin?'

In a corner, he showed me a metal tin with holes which was supposed to attract cockroaches to come to die.

'Never seen any mice.'

I sat on the bed. I looked into his eyes. I tried to see if he had gone mad.

'Why are we here?'

'I wanted to spend the night in an exotic place.'

I realised that he had never really intended to have an orgy here.

He got undressed. He opened the wardrobe to hang up his suit. I saw a pile of men's shirts and underwear on the shelf.

'Are those yours?'

He didn't reply.

He lay on the bed. He snuggled up to me like a child. His back was turned to me. I could hear him sobbing quietly. His arms were clasped around me. I thought of a painting I had seen in an art book at his house. A drowning man hanging on to a rock, which made you wonder what he was doing there in the middle of the waves.

'I'm scared of wolves.'

A childhood phrase that I had heard him say several times in his sleep. He had killed even more wolves than lions. When he was in his honeymoon period with Russian dignitaries, they had taken him to hunt steppe wolves. I went with him once. Massacres that left a landscape of corpses on the red snow. I went back to wait for him in Moscow.

'You have killed so many wolves. You will kill all the wolves.'

Now he was in tears. I knew that he would end up falling asleep like a baby, exhausted from crying.

He snored softly. Every time I tried to get out of his clasp, he held me tighter. I couldn't sleep. I needed a pill. I reached out my hand to my bag on the floor. I touched the strap with the tip of my nail, but I couldn't grab hold of it.

From time to time I heard the sound of a toilet flushing, and soft footsteps on the stairs, as though someone was climbing the stairs holding their shoes in their hands. The room overlooked a silent courtyard. I would have preferred to hear the din of the streets.

He woke up at five o' clock.

'I'll be right back.'

He left the room in his underpants. I heard him go up the stairs. When he got back, he splashed himself with water at the sink.

'You don't want to go to the toilet?'

'No.'

'Are you scared?'

'A bit.'

He came up with me. He waited quietly by the door.

Next, we went to have coffee and *tartines* in the large bar on the corner of the boulevard Barbès. He was calm and cheerful. He talked about the weekend we would soon be spending in Venice at the Danielli.

'For a change, I'll rent a suite on the lagoon.'

That was the only night we ever spent together without any sexual activity.

I didn't ask for any explanation. He didn't offer any. Even today, I don't know why he rented that room. He lived in fear. For him it was probably a hidden den in Paris where he could cower. The police refused to search the hotel. They pretended to believe that it didn't exist.

If his son had agreed to talk at the trial about those three snapshots, the jury would have understood that others were waiting for the right moment to execute him. My act had beaten them to it. I had kept him from martyrdom.

But it was easier to charge me with all responsibility for the murder, on the pretext that I had committed it. Maybe I had preferred to kill him in the act of love to save him from being assassinated in hatred deep in a cave, in a wasteland, a rubbish dump where they would have found him gnawed by rats.

LANDING IN SYDNEY. PASSENGERS FLUNG OFF their blankets like the risen throwing off their shrouds. Agitation of the Last Judgement. I felt weak, and incapable of defending myself in the crush. I huddled in my seat, legs folded up against my chest. Mr Obese had already escaped by making a tunnel with his briefcase.

I had slept a bit at the end of the flight. I started to see the events with more lucidity. Crimes without a culprit do exist. He was condemned, and I had shot like a wife who adds morphine to her husband's drip when he is in the terminal phase, to save him the fright of the last moments. I knew now that I had committed a crime of love. I could be reproached only for having loved him too much.

Getting off the aircraft, the captain smiled at me. I queued at customs. I was taken into the office. I was asked about the purpose of my trip.

'Tourism or business?'

'Business.'

'What is your profession?'

'I'm an artist. I'm here to look for a gallery.'

They emptied the contents of my bag. They smiled when the objects used for his pleasure fell out, which I always kept with me for fear that the maid would find them. A customs officer searched me in a cabin. She didn't find anything. They let me go.

'Have a good stay in Australia.'

'Thank you for your time.'

I was pleased with my English. All winter, I had taken lessons with an American student. When we went on trips, I didn't want to keep embarrassing him with stupid mistakes that showed my lack of higher education.

The airport was spacious enough that groups of travellers didn't crowd together. I could wander around, and look in the shop windows without people bumping into me. I bought an anti-wrinkle cream of a brand unknown in Europe.

I told myself that it was still yesterday, compared to Munich. These hours were like a gift, and I could waste each minute carelessly. In reality, as on the rest of the planet, it was already tomorrow. I knew this when the police pieced together my itinerary.

■

I went into a shop to buy some Marlboros. There was a *New York Times* on the stand next to the counter. His photo was on the front page. The title took up a quarter of the page.

MURDERED
IN LATEX SUIT

I felt dizzy. I crouched down to avoid falling from a height. I lost consciousness. I felt myself being carried. The heels of my boots scraped along the carpet. I opened my eyes again in the stock room. Bundles of newspapers on the floor, and shelves full of cartons of cigarettes.

'Do you feel better?'

'Don't touch me.'

The big man in a baseball cap recoiled. He hadn't touched me, but I was afraid that he might sit on me to immobilise me. I was now aware that the murder had definitely taken place. From this day forward the world's media would echo it incessantly. I was going to have to accept it as a certainty.

I lifted myself up, pushing with the palms of my hands. My head was spinning a bit. The man didn't dare come close to me. I walked into the shop, reaching out with my arms to avoid hitting obstacles whose reflections vibrated like the desert sand at the hottest time of day. I bought the *New York Times* and several Australian papers with names I can't remember. The airport seemed empty, like a pond drained of water and carp. I could only see the walls, and the abandoned counters.

I hid in the toilets. I tore up the photos, the articles, and I put them in the bowl. I almost cried.

Nobody saw me. I had to save my tears to show my grief to his nearest and dearest. I knew his sister, and through her I could no doubt meet the children. Even if it was pathetic, I would hug them one after another to show them that I joined with them in mourning their father. I no longer held it against them that they took the place in his heart that he could have devoted to our child, if he hadn't taken so long to give him to me.

I must have been there a long time. The woman brushing the floor knocked on the cubicle door. I asked what she wanted. She let out a sigh of relief at the fact that I was still alive. A group of young girls came in to ask if they could take a shower anywhere. An old lady complained that there was no disposable toothbrush dispenser. I also heard the noise of cases being rolled, and the rumble of people moving around outside in the hallway.

I left my safe haven. Reality was back. I felt encouraged. I felt sympathy for all the reappeared people. I went back there to make sure that the newspapers hadn't changed their minds. I bought a postcard and a stamp.

I went to sit on a terrace that overlooked the runways. Passing a bar, I saw his photo on a screen. The sound was off. In the foreground, a pair of reporters spoke with the sad smiles that they probably use to announce an earthquake in South America.

The aeroplanes winked in the night. I ordered a cake and a glass of white wine. I called my husband. He told me the news about the murder. I broke down in tears. He was afraid that the police would question my absence. He asked me to come back.

'No, I think I'll be fine here.'

I slid the mobile into my bag to smother his voice. I wrote to my sister to tell her that I was moving to Sydney. Once I'd found a studio, I would send her a plane ticket to come and see me. There were probably landscapes to discover. I had heard that in this continent all the houses had swimming pools and tennis courts.

I went to look for a postbox.

THE TAXI DROVE ALONG THE EDGE OF THE LAKE.

I had posted the card. I had called my husband back. He had already reserved a ticket for me. I went to get it from the Air France counter. I boarded two hours later. We had a stopover in Moscow. I ran into a girl I remembered. She was prettier in her schoolgirl skirt than stuffed into these red leather pants.

'Hello.'

She seemed too cheerful. I didn't respond.

I didn't sleep during the flights. Anxiety proved more powerful than drugs and alcohol.

I watched the water jet, the pale blue sky, the boardwalks on the riverbank where families were having lunch. As usual on a Sunday, the rest of the town was dead. I didn't want to go straight back to the house. My husband was waiting for me on a bench in a square under the battlements.

I rolled down the window. He wasn't looking in my direction. I asked the driver to sound the horn. He arrived, breathing on his glasses to clean them. He tried to kiss me through the open window.

'Hurry up and pay.'

He took a note out of his wallet. He was already annoying me. He waited for the driver to give him the change.

'Keep it.'

He made a motion in the air as if to catch flying coins. I pulled him by the arm before the man selected them one by one from the old sweet tin that he used as a money box.

We walked around the square. There was only one tree, and we got closer to it with every circle we made.

'The police called this morning. They want to see you.'

'I know who killed him.'

He suspected as much. The press mentioned threats made against him. My guilt would not stand up to any enquiry. The truth was made up of many incoherencies, and also this crime looked too much like an assassination to have been committed by a woman.

'As you were close to him, they really have to question you.'

'Let's go home.'

The car was parked on the pavement. A boy on roller-skates told him off for this lack of civility. I was too troubled to get involved.

He talked to me all through the journey. I needed silence.

'I'm not listening. If you don't mind, you can be quiet.'

'Sorry.'

'I need a glass of champagne, a sleeping pill, and my bed.'

'There's no champagne left.'

'Try to find a shop that's open.'

He turned onto the motorway. He was able to buy a bottle at a service station. Waiting for him, I wondered if it might not be better to confess at the first interrogation. The cops would be touched to see me cooperating and admitting to an implausible crime. I would look like I was fabricating, and they would leave me alone for good.

I went to bed straight away. The sleeping pills struggled to put me to sleep. I drank glass after glass, half the bottle. I ended up drinking from the bottle. I woke up at four in the morning. My stomach was burning. I tried to put out the fire by drinking a litre of milk.

My husband was sleeping noisily in the guest room. I went into the garden. It was snowing, the flakes melted in the grass. I went into the barn where I had set up a studio. Since the beginning of the year, I had made a start on large-format works. I had hung one in the dining room. So far, guests had barely commented politely when my husband had asked them to look at it.

I lit the wood stove. I watched the flames through the blackened glass of the door. Perhaps time roasted memories just like funeral pyres roasted corpses. Cinders as light as cigarette ash. When I have forgotten my deed, I will keep only memories of the good moments of our history. It will be as if he were away on a trip. I will even make myself believe in his return.

I was guilty of having shot a giant red doll, just like he used to empty magazines into a portrait of Putin. If he had really been the victim of an attack, he wouldn't have been accused of killing him.

I sat down in front of the painting I had started the week before. Traces of blue, and a piece of green silk stuck in the centre. I tried to draw his face by dipping my finger in black paint. I managed to make a sinister figure whose snout-like nose made his head look more like the head of a boar.

To get a break, he advised me to do erotic paintings.

'You will come to the opening in a basque.'

'They'll think I'm a whore.'

HE HAD ALWAYS KEPT ME UNDER SURVEILLANCE. I noticed once that my post had been opened, or that a stranger surreptitiously photographed me in the street. But since the end of the previous year, before the spring of the murder, I was followed day and night. I even suspected him of having had me wiretapped by order of the minister who we'd dined with a year earlier.

One morning in February, I had been the victim of an assassination attempt. I was en route to Paris. A BMW coupé that had just overtaken me started zigzagging in front of me. The passenger door opened, and the torso of an armed man appeared. He fired a burst up and down. The bullets went into the sky, hit the wheels, the roof, ricocheted off the asphalt. I veered onto the hard shoulder. I managed to escape by reversing.

The judge deemed that my story was not believable. He forbade the stenographer from noting it down.

'I think the lady is tired.'

He rang the bell for the police to take me back to prison.

■

Since he sequestered my money, I had cut him off. Like a couple divorcing who haggle over the children, I only wanted to speak to him through my lawyer.

'What children?'

'The ones you haven't given me yet.'

'You've gone completely crazy.'

'You'll have to talk to my lawyer.'

'What lawyer?'

Ashamed to mention my husband's obscure little lawyer, who I had to put up with for financial reasons, I had given him the name of a star of the bar who I had seen on television the night before. He called me back to say that he had just phoned him.

'He's never heard of you.'

'Why did you call him? You could have trusted me.'

He laughed at the other end of the line.

'Are you mocking me?'

I hung up.

Two days before the murder, he had left sobs on my answerphone. The tears of a child in a state of desperation, like the ones he cried sometimes at night in my arms, telling me he was scared of wolves. I wondered if I had been attacked on the motorway by the killers who would soon deal with him.

■

He came to our house at nine-thirty in the evening. He parked his Bentley in the drive. I was closing my bedroom shutters. I saw him cross the garden. I locked myself in the bathroom. I wasn't scared of him. I dreaded that he had come to escape those who wanted his scalp.

My husband opened the door to him. I heard them talk. I heard the voice of a man in danger. He cried out phrases like he was shouting for help. My husband answered with a calm and muted voice. Like a police commissioner sent to negotiate with a madman. There was a movement towards the stairs, then a scuffle. My husband raised his voice. He calmed down, he left. I heard the Bentley skid on the gravel.

I came down. My husband was sitting in a chair. Leaning on the table, he held his head as if it might roll onto the patio like a boule. I came closer to him. For the first time in several years, I placed my hand on his shoulder. He turned his eyes towards me. He looked grateful, and his mouth was wet like a muzzle.

'You should agree to see him.'

'The lawyer sent him a letter.'

'I'm worried he'll kill himself. The family will accuse you of having driven him to it.'

'I want him to give up. So he stops choosing his money over our love.'

'What if he puts a bullet in his head?'

I didn't want his children to be able to hold his suicide against me. I had seen a documentary about the children of suicides. They try to kill themselves when they reach the age that their father died. A tear had rolled onto my cheek. He tried to console me. I moved away.

'Please.'

'I'm sorry.'

We were out of champagne again. There was just a drop of whisky in the bottle. I found a flask of kirsch that I had bought to make a cake. I wanted to save him having to spend fifty euros at a patisserie.

'Why are you drinking from the bottle? Imagine if someone saw you.'

I gave a kick in the air to show him that I didn't give a fuck. He smiled.

'You're right, I'm an old fool.'

I found it annoying to be with such a mature man. If he had enjoyed a different social status the age difference wouldn't count. It would even be admirable to be able to keep, at the age of thirty-seven, a wealthy husband who could have married a top model as colourless as a gravestone. I tried to throw the flask into the bin. It rolled under the sideboard.

'I need to get that money back.'

'Tell him that otherwise I will forbid you to see him.'

I burst out laughing. I imagined him grounding me like a schoolgirl, banning me from using the phone to keep me from talking to him.

'You're talking crap.'

'My banker calls every day. He's going to take a mortgage on the house to cover my overdraft.'

'You should have been a surgeon.'

He left the kitchen with his tail between his legs. I imagined his penis shrivelling up in his 'Monday' underpants. I had given him a whole set on his birthday. A day of the week was stamped in red on each of them, on the buttocks.

'Don't get the wrong day.'

'I'll be careful.'

He was always moved when I gave him a present.

He wandered into the doorway.

'He would like to have dinner with you tomorrow.'

'I'm going to call him.'

'Just send him a message. He's reserved a table for eight-thirty.'

A RESTAURANT BUILT ON AN ISLAND OF DECKING, reached by a wooden bridge. An impression of being in the middle of the lake. Just like in his office at La Défense that overlooked Paris, he must have felt like he was the centre of the world.

To him, I was just a twig. A free mistress, confirming to him the low opinion he'd always had of women. My role as a sexual secretary reduced me to the rank of a beater at the shoot. I was no longer certain of the love which had until then been the only reward for my devotion. Maybe his penchant for men had made him a true invert. I suspected that there was a lover somewhere, someone he genuinely loved.

He had reserved an isolated corner. I wondered if he had ordered them to remove tables to create a little islet within the island. I was there half an hour early, to have time to drink champagne before he arrived. I didn't have the strength to face him sober. When he arrived, I had just ordered a second bottle.

'You won't kiss me?'

I gave him a kiss on each cheek.

'You're very nice.'

He looked me up and down like a horse trader.

'You should eat something other than Lexomil. You look like an anorexic.'

I got up to leave.

'You can barely stand up.'

I let myself fall back onto my chair.

'You despise me.'

'Oh really? I don't know why I would take the trouble.'

He called the maître d'. He ordered foie gras and two chateaubriands.

'How would you like it?'

'Very rare.'

He knew well that I hated the taste of blood. I only like meat that is grey from stewing. He showed his teeth.

'Bitches like raw meat.'

I started to cry. Tears played an important role in his life. The ones he cried allowed him to recover his fantasy of the child maltreated by his mother. A strange arousal, beyond the desire for suffering, of domination. When he stared into that abyss, he no longer even sought any sexual contact. His penis retracted, as if it too sought to go back to the beginning of the 1960s, when his mother washed him in cold water in the old painted bathtub in a mansion in Neuilly. A dream he wallowed in while awake. A nightmare that woke him at night.

He had asked me to find this unloved child. A miserable child, a reminiscence, a memory that forty years later he could still touch with his finger. I'd had to endure the categorical refusal of a friend whose son I had wanted to borrow. The concierge of a hotel in Saint Petersburg had found a little Slav for me. So that he'd resemble him, I had dyed his blond hair raven black.

A surprise he had found in the bathroom when he came home one evening after a meeting with a wheeler-dealer who is today a guest at a work camp in Siberia. I undressed him, and got him to stand on a stool, as on a pedestal. He walked around him without daring to touch him, nor to speak to him in the few words of Russian he knew. They both had the same anxious stare.

'Send him back.'

'He cost a fortune.'

I took him back to the hotel bar where his mother was waiting for him. She was badly dressed, and the barman had already asked her several times to leave.

He also liked my tears. An intense pleasure at seeing them flow. Proof of his power, as if he were a god inflicting the rain. As soon as my gaze became misty, his penis would stand up. It became even harder than in the evenings when he took stimulants to counteract the side effects of the antidepressants, prescribed at Sainte Anne hospital to stop him lying on his office couch letting his business go down the drain.

He had asked me one morning to accompany him to the hospital. A waiting room with brown flock wallpaper, worn out, hanging on the walls for more than thirty years, and with holes from cigarettes stubbed out by lunatics back when hospitals were as smoky as gaming rooms. A reedy loudspeaker called for the patients, whether tramps or television presenters. They put up with this humiliation in order to see a leading expert who had never agreed to open a private practice. A short man, with hands that were so hairy they were almost black, and who refused the money of stars hoping for clandestine visits in the intimacy of their homes.

'Are you crying?'

'You're making me cry.'

He got a better hard-on when I admitted that he was responsible for the shower. Even in public, he couldn't help letting his finger slide along the corners of my eyes to taste my tears close to their source. If we were alone, he would drink them straight from the skin. He liked me to jerk him off at the same time.

When I caught sight of the waiter, I dried my eyes with my napkin. I don't really like foie gras. I swallowed one gulp and then a second one so that he could enjoy my retching. The meat arrived, I cut off a piece and chewed it with my mouth open, for him to see the blood spurt.

'You have red chops.'

I knew he was going to come. A chuckle, and then the dampness that reminded him of his soaked pyjamas every night until he was eighteen years old.

I had him. At that moment, his penis would fall like a dead weight, and domination would change sides. He didn't resist me any more; I would feel his need to crawl, to try to cling to my legs every time I gave him a kick with my boot. He was suffering because he couldn't be locked up in a room, where, with the look of a frightened child, he would beg me to spare him.

I went for him.

'You're going to give me the money back.'

He was struggling. A murmur.

'No.'

'Well, keep it then. My lawyer will send you a quit-claim.'

He whimpered. A victim who is suddenly spared torture.

'But tomorrow morning at eleven o'clock, you'll wait for me in front of the bank. You'll ask for one million dollars in cash at the counter. We'll go to the toilets. You'll pull down your trousers. You'll bite the wads, one after the other. I'll pull them from you and use them to wipe the dribble from your chin. Then I'll clench your bollocks in my hands. You'll be ashamed of coming. Cum will flow like drivel from your flabby prick.'

He was crying. The head waiter brought him the bill. He gave him an earful, turning his teary face towards the lake.

'Are you throwing us out?'

'I'm sorry, I made a mistake. I thought you had waved to me to ask for the bill.'

'For the trouble, tell the manager that tonight I won't pay.'

'I'm sincerely sorry.'

'Get the hell away.'

'With all my apologies, sir. I wish you an excellent evening.'

He walked away with small steps to avoid irritating him by rapping the planks with his shoes.

'The pig.'

'Are you insulting the servants?'

'I didn't ask him for anything.'

'Open your mouth.'

'Why?'

'Obey.'

With a surreptitious look around me, I checked that no one was looking at us. I took his tongue between my nails. I pulled it, and I waited for him to squeak like a trapped mouse before letting go of it. I wish I could have entered him like acid, so that he would end up pissing me out with a yell.

I stood up.

'See you tomorrow.'

I couldn't make out his face against the backlighting of the moon. Then he dropped this phrase that I decided never to forgive.

'One million dollars; that's expensive for a whore.'

On the following day, I waited in vain for him in front of the bank. My husband had parked in the underground car park. We drove back home. We sat in the kitchen. He was chewing crumbs from the pieces of toast scattered around the breakfast bowls.

'I'm going to send his son all the photos I left at my uncle's place.'

ON THE DAY AFTER MY RETURN FROM AUSTRALIA, I went to the main police station not to excite suspicion by waiting for them to call me in. I was met by two inspectors.

'Please sit down.'

I was feeling nervous.

'Can I light a cigarette?'

They were hesitant. The old one ended up allowing me to do so, with a nod.

'Did you see the victim on the day of the murder?'

I denied it. But they had viewed the CCTV film.

'When I saw him, he was already dead. He was locked inside a latex suit. A bit like the bags they put dead people in, in TV series. I couldn't even be sure that it was him. I heard some noise in the back of the apartment. Male voices, speaking a strange language. They must have been looking for something.'

'For what?'

'Everybody knew he was condemned. He was expecting to be executed. He didn't care. He used to say that he wasn't fond enough of life to be afraid of losing it.

You can check; he was seeing a psychiatrist. I'm sure he'll tell you there was nothing that could cure him. Some untreated childhood stuff that was eroding him all his life. Now it had spread. Had he not been shot down, he would have killed himself. He loved guns; the only way he wanted to die was with a bullet in the head.'

'Did he tell you so?'

'He played Russian roulette a lot.'

They were suspicious. The old one took off his glasses. He tapped his left eye nervously. From the noise it was making, it seemed to me that it was a glass eye.

'He didn't commit suicide. We didn't find the gun.'

'Then, someone must have killed him.'

I thrust my hand into my bag to take a pill. I sucked it like a sweet.

'You must find the murderers.'

They both laughed, a little mocking laugh, like the call of the blackbird in Avallon that woke me up every morning.

'He probably didn't have the courage to kill himself. Maybe he paid them to murder him.'

They didn't believe me. I felt like asking them what they'd like me to tell them.

'Why didn't you call the police?'

'I was afraid of the reprisals. I thought I'd better go far away.'

The old one put up a finger, like a harpoon thrown to catch one of the questions buzzing around the room like hornets.

'And this latex suit, did you know about it?'

'He was very secretive. He was leading a double life, dozens of lives. He didn't know which one to choose. He was always disappointed, all the time trying new ones.'

They looked at each other. Like accomplices. Two boys who are about to shout dirty things at a girl. The young one leafed through the folder that was lying on the computer keyboard.

'We found an old email from the third of June 2002.'

'We used to send each other a lot of messages. He would outline his fantasies, and for my part I would tell him how we had achieved them together.'

'But actually, they weren't true?'

'Obviously.'

'On the third of June, you wrote that you had just bought him a latex suit "to play". You even specified that "they had to order it, they didn't have one big enough in stock."'

'He was very tall; he would only wear made-to-measure suits.'

'But you're the one who bought it, aren't you?'

I was afraid they would take me into custody. I preferred to acquiesce.

'Anyway, I paid for it. When I put it on him, he felt safe from reality. It was reality that frightened him. He saw it more or less as a forest. He believed there were wild animals behind the trees. That's why he enjoyed hunting so much. But he knew he would never be able to kill them all, there would always be some left. They're protected species, so they reproduce. When I put the latex suit on him, he was like a baby from the Middle Ages. You know, like in those paintings where their whole bodies are swaddled. I became like his nanny. I protected him; I was the whole world to him. He was no longer afraid.'

'Did you engage in sadomasochistic sessions with him?'

They both had the shiny look of vicious men.

'That's an overstatement.'

They were smiling, quietly ironic. I couldn't bear that they were mocking him.

'What about you? What do you do? You surely have a wife? A boyfriend? Penetration is sadomasochism too. There has to be one person above the other, anyway.'

I stood up.

'I had been told that in this country, policemen were more polite than French cops.'

They didn't let me go. They wanted to talk to me about this million dollars, of which I hadn't seen a single cent. I didn't feel like cooperating with them any more. I gave an evasive answer.

'Anyway, that money never changed our love at all.'

As I walked out of the police station, I called his sister. The children had arrived two days before with their mother. She had already got a psychology unit to support them. A team whose phone number she had been given by the health minister. Usually, they were sent to take care of the passengers' families when an aeroplane crashed.

'I'd like to see the children.'

The therapist who was taking care of the eldest son specifically wanted him to see me. He often mentioned my name, as if I were a shadow in his father's life that prevented him from keeping a vivid image of him.

'Come right away.'

She was living in the hills above the city. Photographers were hanging around the building. She had hired security guards to guard the entrance. They called her before letting me in. She opened the door. She'd had her hair cut since we last met, three weeks before.

'You were right to get rid of that fringe.'

She fell into my arms.

'You were so close. You must be devastated.'

'I was on holiday in Sydney. I came back in a hurry.'

I sobbed. She took me into the bathroom so that I could wipe my tears away. I made myself up again.

'They're in the living room.'

She held my hand while we were crossing the hall.

'I'll leave you here.'

I entered the room by myself. The three children were sitting on the sofa. The psychologists had decided not to attend the meeting. The mother greeted me coldly. She left, taking the two youngest with her, without even giving me time to say hello.

I found myself alone with the eldest. His face was almost white, but he had always had a pale complexion. His eyes were almost black from insomnia and were not reddened by tears. I felt that his father's death was making an adult of him. He was imperceptibly becoming the head of this family that had been devastated by divorce ten years earlier.

'You're brave.'

I wanted to sit by his side. He could have lain down and put his head on my lap. A recollection of the evenings we had spent together in Paris. We would have found some serenity, the few minutes of quiet that we both needed, to find the strength to go through this ordeal.

But he stood up as I came near. I didn't hold his gaze. He went to the window. He turned his back on me without a word.

'I don't know what to say to you. This is so sad.'

I was standing behind him. I could hear him breathing with the same deep inhalations as his father's on days when I felt he was about to go for my throat to tear it open with his teeth, like a wild animal.

I left the living room, trying not to run. I ran in the hall, bumping into the mother who was listening at the door. Outside, the photographers were forming a line on each side of the porch. It was still daylight, but they dazzled me with their flashes.

As I arrived home, for the first time in my life I felt cold sweat running down my back.

I WAS CALLED IN BY THE COPS THREE TIMES A week, for about two weeks. Insistent questionings. They always wanted more details about our relationship.

'I don't have anything to say to you.'

'In a message from the twenty-first of March 2004, he promised he would marry you.'

'I didn't accept. I'm already married, and I will never get divorced.'

This time, they had not allowed me to light a cigarette. I had asked for a break to go and smoke outside, but they had carried on harassing me without even bothering to answer.

'Your wedding in Las Vegas has no legal status.'

'Besides, on the third of April, you reminded him of his promise.'

They were subjecting me to a crossfire of questions.

'You demanded the million dollars after his revocation, "as proof of your love".'

'One million dollars is a strange way to demonstrate love.'

'He was avaricious. When he agreed, I understood that he loved me. I was worth something; I was as precious to him as the sketchbook by Picasso that he had bought in October in Drouot. It's an exchange, love. I had given my whole self to him, and it really was all I had. He could easily give me a million. It was a minuscule part of his fortune. As if I had cut a lock of my hair for him to wear in a locket.'

They both stood up from their seats. They came nearer. Their faces were above me, their four eyes gazing into mine.

'Did you kill him?'

'I don't think so.'

'So, you killed him?'

'No, it's impossible. I couldn't want to kill him. I don't like to kill, apart from birds at the hunt, small game. But him, he killed mammals. Even elephants. He was always armed; he could easily have shot me like an animal.'

'You didn't kill him then?'

'To my mind, I didn't kill him. I'm almost certain of it. If you have proof of my killing him, please tell me. But it won't mean that I'm lying. Innocents have been condemned before because there was proof of their guilt.'

'And if we found it, this piece of evidence?'

'I'd confess; I wouldn't be able to do otherwise.'

They went back to their seats. The old one was smiling, the young one was typing.

'Beware if I confess, though. People even give themselves up for killing someone who is still alive.'

He printed the text that he had just typed.

'Please sign your statement.'

'And then I'll be able to leave?'

'Yes.'

I needed a cigarette and a drink. I signed. He snatched the sheet out of my hand.

'We'll see you again on Friday at two o'clock.'

'Do you still suspect me?'

The young one laughed. The old one spoke with the soft voice of a nurse who is talking to a schizophrenic.

'Not at all. But we'll be very happy to see you again.'

'Two o'clock isn't good for me. I have an appointment with my masseur in the late morning. I'd like to have time to eat a sandwich before coming.'

'We'll prepare dinner for you.'

I was fed up. I didn't see the point of letting him know that it was not a time to have dinner.

'See you on Friday.'

'I might be fifteen or twenty minutes late.'

SINCE RETURNING FROM AUSTRALIA, I COULDN'T find any peace. I wanted to hear his voice. I would call his mobile for the pleasure of listening to his message. I would wait for the beep and then stay with the silence. I would remain silent, for fear his ex-wife was monitoring his voicemail.

I was trying to divert myself. I had forced my husband to take me to the cinema, and to jog with me in the street, hoping that this would release enough endorphins to befuddle me. Tranquillizers didn't ease the pain, neither did champagne.

I contacted friends who I had not seen for a long time. They pitied me for finding myself at the centre of this case. I was trying to convince them that this murder had been inevitable. There are countries where you cannot go into business with impunity. A war declared between the East and the West. Russians as cruel as Afghans. A permanent, insidious attack, with collapsing stock markets and beheaded hostages.

'I might confess. Only to be safe in jail, however long it takes for the United States to crush them. I'll live an ordered life. I'll do sports. I'll register for a pottery class. I'll learn languages, history, accountancy. It will be exactly the same as if I were a student at university. I'll leave prison with a degree. Degrees are important.'

'You should see a doctor.'

'I'm seeing plenty of them. I don't want to run out of drugs.'

'You should stop.'

'If I'm arrested, I'll be in peace for many years. With my million dollars, I'll be able to buy strawberries and cherries in the middle of winter from the prison shop. I'll ask for a cell with a view of the lake. At weekends the teachers will take us out to get some fresh air. I'll finally learn to ski.'

Today I realise what a state of mental confusion I was in. I didn't feel safe anywhere. Sometimes I was so afraid of being followed that I left the car in the middle of the road. I would walk around and get lost in the alleys of the old town. I would look for a church where I could kneel down. I cried before the cross. I was telling myself that a convent might be like the Legion. I would be given another name. The police would not look for me there.

I was seeing my Indian masseur every day. I surrendered myself completely naked to him. I left my anxiety and my clothes on the chair. I lay down. The table was covered with a linen sheet. He did not need to tie me up. I put myself under his protection. His hands infused in me the serenity that life had never granted. My past was buried somewhere, the future shut in a bank's safety deposit box that I would never ask to be opened. The present smelled like jasmine in the half-light of the candles.

When the session ended, I begged him to keep me longer.

'My next client is waiting.'

I took his arm. I kissed it. It didn't quiver.

'Are you homosexual?'

He smiled. A Sphinx's smile.

'See you tomorrow, madam.'

I put my clothes back on.

'You're the only person I feel good with.'

'Ask your husband to prescribe herbal medicine for you.'

I left.

MY HUSBAND HAD PREPARED THE COFFEE-MAKER. I only had to press the button and the coffee would start flowing. I was about to leave. I was looking at the garden with the eyes of somebody who is leaving. A long stay, not a holiday, but rather a sort of course of treatment in a gloomy spa, with stingy and rare rays of sunlight. I was not sad; after all I knew that I would not spend my life there.

I took my time in the bathroom. A toning face mask. A scalp massage with essential oils. A wax. A long shower. I mopped the excess water from my hair with a towel. I let it dry naturally. I made myself up with the products I had bought on the plane coming back from Australia.

I stayed for a while in front of the wardrobe. I put on light underwear, ecru cotton. No stockings, it was too hot. A lavender-blue blouse, a little black skirt, and a pair of flat shoes. I went to get my suitcase from the cellar. It got full very fast. I also filled an overnight bag.

I made a flying visit to the studio. I didn't touch the painting. I would finish it later. I would have improved my drawing by then. I left the door wide open. A bit of wind would clear the atmosphere that was saturated with the smells of paint. My husband would shut it when he came back.

He had taken the car to go to his office. I was dropped off by a cab at the masseur's. I left my luggage in the waiting room.

'Are you leaving for Avallon?'

'Yes, I want a rest.'

'You need it.'

I undressed. I knew he would be the last man to touch my body for a long time. He would not massage me the next day, or the next year. I was already missing it.

I did not get up on the table.

'Are you getting dressed again?'

'I'm scared my plane may leave early.'

'At best, they leave on time.'

He was surprised that I kissed him on the mouth. Furtively, as I had seen certain parents do with their child.

It was only midday. I balanced the bag on the suitcase and had a walk, dragging it along behind me, like a tourist getting lost in an unknown town. A young man asked me if he could help me.

'Are you looking for your hotel?'

'No, I'm in transit.'

He bought me a drink at a café terrace. The lake was just across the road, calm, with no boats. I could not hear very well what he was telling me because of the traffic noise. I was looking at people walking by. They seemed upset, with their phones to their ears. They started to laugh, then they hung up and dispersed like a crowd at the end of a demonstration.

'Would you like to have a salad?'

He had raised his voice so that I could hear him.

'Where do you live?'

My question frightened him.

'I don't know.'

'Where?'

'Not far from here.'

He dragged my suitcase for me all the way to his one-room flat.

'Would you like an orange juice?'

I smiled.

'I want you to have sex with me.'

'I don't think so.'

I took him in my arms. He struggled.

'Leave me alone.'

'Why don't you want to?'

'I don't feel like it.'

'You are the one who approached me.'

He sat on the bed.

'I like to chat with mature women.'

If I'd had him when I was sixteen, I could have been his mother. You don't have sex with your son, he was right to call me to order.

'Can you take me out?'

'My motorbike was stolen last Sunday.'

'We'll walk.'

We dilly-dallied in the town. We passed an ice cream shop. I slipped a note into his hand.

'Can you buy me a vanilla cone?'

He gave me my change, like an honest child sent grocery shopping. We went through a shopping mall. I took him into a shoe shop.

'Let me buy you navy-blue moccasins.'

He did not protest. He kept them on and threw away his old Nikes in the umbrella stand that he took for a bin.

After the shop, I still had some time.

'What about having lunch?'

I took him to a restaurant. I ordered oysters and champagne.

'We'll never drink the whole bottle.'

'You'll take it back home.'

I only downed one glass. I didn't want to arrive there drunk. He ate almost all the oysters. I was not hungry. I raised one to my lips. I wanted to drink its juice. To taste the sea in my mouth.

'Aren't you eating anything?'

'I'm on a diet.'

'You're already so thin.'

It was one forty-five. I didn't have time to ask for the bill. I stood up.

'Are you not paying?'

'I'm in too much of a hurry. Go first with the suitcase.'

'Seriously?'

'Hurry up.'

He obeyed. I waited until he had gone ahead. I went out at a leisurely pace. Once I was outside, I speeded up. No one chased me. I found him hidden behind a bus stop.

'You're a bit eccentric.'

'A bit mad?'

'Yes.'

I had a strange feeling when I saw the police station. Like a gloomy travel agency. I would not choose the destination, and I would be despatched like freight.

'Are you a cop?'

I ran my hand in his curly hair.

'Don't be scared.'

The sentry watched us enter with my luggage. I sat next to a couple full of hatred towards a stranger who had burgled their house while they were at a stretching class in a sports club.

'You can leave.'

I kissed him several times on his forehead. He was standing in front of me, his arms crossed, awkward, smiling.

'Go.'

'Goodbye then.'

He left, slowly putting one moccasin before the other, as if he wasn't sure he wanted to leave. He didn't backtrack.

I WAS THREE MINUTES EARLY. THE INSPECTORS came to pick me up at exactly two o'clock. They seemed annoyed when they saw the suitcase.

'You're on bail, you're not allowed to leave the country.'

'I came to give myself up.'

They gave a high five, as if they were congratulating each other on having won a juicy contract. They made me enter the office.

'Sit down. We're going to get everything in black and white.'

'I forgot to take my luggage.'

'It's safe.'

'And you won't need all that crap in jail anyway.'

They would have liked a detailed confession. I was tired from three years of love. Our relationship had never been serene. A passion lived in a state of panic. A murder whose only beneficiaries would eventually be the children, once they had overcome their grief.

Everything was over now. I did not want to make the effort to remember. Besides, at that point, my memory was blurred. Events were floating in a mass of chaos, like the cargo of a schooner sunk by pirates.

I had let them talk, telling the story for me. They seemed delighted that I didn't interrupt them or butt in. Before I signed, I still had some phrases modified that were too damning. I agreed in advance to sacrifice a part of my life, but I would have found it unfair to spend decades in jail.

IN A CELL, THE YEARS GO BY SLOWLY. YOU HAVE time to tidy your belongings. A few clothes that you wash in the small sink. Eyeshadow, lipstick, that you use on the days when you have visitors. Magazines where you can see close-up pictures of stars' cellulite. A notebook to write poems or whatever. Drawing paper covered with sketches. A personal stereo to hammer music into your head and drown the noise of the TV switched on at eight o'clock in the morning by your cellmate and only switched off late in the evening at curfew.

Time clears the memory. A picture whose varnish has darkened. A remorseless scrubbing. Then the truth appears as neat as a Jérôme Bosch painting.

His apartment was dotted with caches of arms. In each room you could find a gun within reach, barely hidden, in a vase of dried flowers, in an old wig box from the seventeenth century, or carelessly left under a sofa like a lighter that slipped from someone's hands. In the lounge, a .22 rifle hung behind a Quattrocento triptych. In his bedroom there was a 9mm in each of his bedside tables. In the end, the fear of being murdered by killers had ended up making his passion for weapons useful.

On the evening of the murder, I entered his place with my key. It was already dark. I went into the bathroom to get changed. A short black vinyl dress. Stockings that made my legs look like fish caught in nets. I put my high-heeled boots back on.

The bedroom was adjoining. I spread the latex suit on the bed. I put the hood on it so that he would think of a dead man. I placed a chair in the centre of the room. I opened the first drawer of the chest of drawers. Inside the wooden quilted casket where he kept some accessories that we used during our sessions was a revolver the same as the one he had given me as a present two years before. A revolver whose cylinder was empty and that had become just another sex toy. I replaced it with mine. I rolled the other up in a towel. I went to the kitchen. I threw it down the rubbish chute. An act that seems absurd to me today. It must have ended up in the rubbish dump the following day. The police never found it.

I opened the fridge. I put my hand on a bottle of Dom Pérignon. I took a can of Coca-Cola. I was afraid of the indulgence that is sometimes brought on by intoxication. I sat on the terrace in front of the tiny swimming pool that was little more than a jacuzzi. Above the lights of the docks, the phosphorescent water jet was spouting like dust in the middle of the grey lake.

At the beginning of the afternoon, I had looked at the train schedule. I wanted to go and get the photographs and bring them to his son the next day. I had called my uncle.

'Go and fetch them from the safe right now.'

'Will you spend the night at our place this time?'

'I'm not coming.'

I had changed my mind. I preferred that he die. I took the revolver. I went to his company's building. The girl at the reception desk recognised me.

'Don't announce me, he's expecting me.'

I arrived on the fifteenth floor. I barged past his assistant. He was alone in his office. I dug my hand into my bag. I caught the handle of the revolver.

He was not even surprised to see me.

'This morning, I totally forgot the bank thing.'

He was enjoying taking the piss out of me. An off-hand throaty voice, barely articulated words. Contempt.

'If you like, we can see each other tonight at my place. We'll have a little impromptu dinner?'

My finger was on the trigger. I raised my arm.

'What are you doing with your bag up in the air?'

RÉGIS JAUFFRET

I tried not to look at his face. To shoot right in his heart, the way he had taught me to make a hole in a cardboard target. I could not press. I understood that I would never be able to shoot a man. During the sessions, I could imagine that there was nobody under the suit.

The hour of his death was coming to depend on traffic jams, on the speed of his steps in the car park, on the lift that would take a long time going down despite the repeated thumb raps on the call button. I would need twenty minutes to talc him, and to mould his body slowly into the latex.

He arrived. He did not dare to say a word. He could see in my eyes that, tonight, I had agreed to take him over. An immediate erection, and the sperm I stole during the little death.

I motioned him to make for the bedroom. I undressed him. I coated him with talc. A funeral ablution. I was feeling the same peace as on the day of an Ashkenazi friend's funeral when I listened to the rabbi reciting the Kaddish. I dressed him slowly, with the precaution of an embalmer. He was inert, pacified, surrendered to my soft and sweet-scented hands, whose long nails had hurt his tongue – the mark was still there. I slipped the hood

164

over his head. As I pulled the zip, he uttered a moan, a sigh on the verge of pleasure.

A mummy lying on the bed. Incongruous, exiled far from its mastaba, from its pyramid, from the hole in the sand where grave plunderers buried it out of superstition after having taken from it the small offering that would have allowed it to pay its crossing of the Styx, if by some chance humans are not deprived of the beyond.

'Stand up.'

I pulled him delicately. I took him to the chair.

'Here.'

He sat. I took the rope. He reacted.

'Calm down.'

He did not like being tied up.

'It's only to prevent you from falling.'

I fastened the clasp. He let his arms fall. He let fear, euphoria, anxiety, happiness rise in him. He knew the moment was coming when the governess would get angry, and threaten him with death.

He heard me opening the chest of drawers, the casket. I took the revolver. I came nearer. I pulled back the hammer. A familiar noise. I spun the cylinder. I felt him trembling. I put the barrel delicately between his eyes. He let out a lascivious moan.

A dummy. An unknown man. An animal in its shell. A pest, enormous, ludicrous and pink like a baby girl's clothes. I shot.

I WAS TAKEN OUT FROM MY CELL AT TWO O'CLOCK in the afternoon. My husband was waiting for me in the visiting room.

He says he will no longer be in debt when I get out of jail. Maybe he thinks that I will not be released before the end of my prison term. Last week, my lawyer promised me that his application for a provisional release would succeed.

'I'll be out in a month.'

'Good.'

He looked concerned. His financial situation was probably not any healthier yet.

'I'll work, you know.'

'Yes, of course. But unemployment is very high at the moment.'

'Especially among former convicts.'

He lowered his head, mumbling. I made a sign to the warder who was on guard duty behind the window.

'I'm going to leave.'

He shook his head.

'I just arrived.'

'I can't miss the priest's visit.'

He was jealous of the relationship I had forged with this man. He had made me realise how right I was to believe in God. I had confessed my entire life to him, he had given me absolution.

'So it's as if this story had happened to somebody else?'

He had closed his eyes.

'It's as if it hadn't happened at all?'

He was about to answer me. I placed my finger on his lips.

OTHER TITLES FROM
SALAMMBO PRESS

WWW.SALAMMBOPRESS.COM

LACRIMOSA

Régis Jauffret

Lacrimosa unfolds through a moving exchange of letters between the narrator and his young lover, Charlotte, who has just committed suicide. Their poignant dialogue makes this epistolary novel a truly cathartic experience.

—

Lacrimosa is marked by Jauffret's own direct involvement in both the real-life events and the narrative, an internal exploration deepened by his own experience.

Russell Williams, *TLS*

Lacrimosa works like a literary boxing match, a heartbreaking masterpiece where emotion is never far from the absurd. ***L'Express***

Tragic and caustic. *Télérama*

Régis Jauffret has perhaps written his most accomplished novel, a work of devastating and devastated beauty: an ode to a dead lover. ***Le Magazine Littéraire***

If you follow my advice, I promise: while reading *Lacrimosa*, you will both endure enjoyment and suffering. *Lacrimosa* is just made of what life is made of. **Vice Versa**

A savage epistolary dialogue made for a great novel.
Nouvel Observateur

A merciless tale in which honesty explodes from every page, sometimes to the point of provocation. **Figaro**

THÉRÈSE
AND ISABELLE
Violette Leduc

Charged with metaphors, alternating with precise descriptions of sensations and human relationships, *Thérèse and Isabelle* was censored by its publisher in France in 1954, first published in a truncated version in 1966 and not until 2000 in its uncensored edition, as Violette Leduc intended.

For the first time in a new English translation, this is the unabridged text of *Thérèse and Isabelle*.

—

Thérèse and Isabelle is written with unflinching sincerity and Leduc's progressive attitude and experimental style confirm it as one of the greatest examples of French-language erotic literature.
Olivia Heal, *TLS*

If the uncensored Thérèse and Isabelle reads like a fever-dream, to many it represents a long-awaited panacea.
Thea Lenarduzzi, *Literary Review*

Here we have extraordinary writing about sex; and, more importantly, about love, and the way it makes us feel.
Nicholas Lezard, *Guardian*

Thunderbolts of illicit love. A classy new translation of Leduc's masterpiece on the tyranny of love.   *Independent*

Reading Leduc is like discovering a whole new nervous system.
Deborah Levy

THE UNIVERSE EXPLAINED TO MY GRANDCHILDREN

Hubert Reeves

"Grandpa, how big is the universe? How far are the stars? How can we tell the sun's age? Are we stardust? What is thunder? Is the universe expanding? Do black holes exist? What is the future of the universe?"

In this book, master astrophysicist Hubert Reeves unlocks the secrets of the universe. This is his spiritual testament to younger generations and a perfect occasion for us all to revise our conceptions about the cosmos.

―

Reeves' fascination with the history and ultimate fate of the universe, and with the role we play as a conscious part of it, is beautiful and infectious. The reader gets a taste for the history and philosophy, as well as the facts, of science, and the conversational tone makes these very complex ideas accessible to teenagers and adults alike.   *I, Science*